First Published in 2011 by teresamcloughlin.

First edition

ISBN 978-0-9568605-0-7

Forward

The novel is a story of a baby developing during a season of hurricanes, and how her personality becomes set through the information she hears. The information comes to her through the television, internet, history and her genes. The book contains chrystian theology, moles and maps, sociology and anthropology, pyramids and palms, conspiracy and cults; hardly any of it is true.

The novel was inspired by my own skin condition, which doctors haven't been able to diagnose. I was born with a slight hand shape to my face, with a fate line along one side of my brow. Every summer a shadow appears by my nose, in the shape of a snail. I also have a permanent birth mark, in the shape of a face, on my forehead. I share other blemishes with the character in the novel, but I must stress that it is fictional.

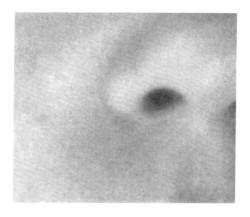

Chapter 1

Pray.

Put the hands together above the bed clothes, and pray. It is not a sin to masturbate, but it is a sign of stupidity. They rely on the old nightly ritual of prayer to stop them reaching for warmth between their legs when they are asleep and too cold to know what their hands do by instinct, which is to scratch and curl. Pointless routine is a well known trainer of the subconscious, they think.

Their feet are soaked in athlete's foot. The skin in between the toes splits and bleeds, protesting at unaccustomed exercise as the newly formed adolescents add their efforts in the fields. The infection turns and squirms at the top of the thigh, and grows in proportion to fit a fairy mushroom circle of ring worm. It is a fungal flight of fantasy. The hands reach between the toes, then between the thighs. The ring worm slips around the creases of the pubes, emerging with broken bacterial wings and sloping, limping, its pattern of circles.

And breathe in and breathe out the microscopic shit from the air of butterflies, wasp, and horse flies. They are defecating and ovulating as they flitter in between the greenery. The air is full of them. They hover above, unseen by the naked eye; miles of daddy long legs, beetles, and mosquitoes, breeding and pissing. The bacteria off them nest in the lungs as if the alveoli were tree branches. They will grow into fur balls of phlegm and split sensitive linings.

Remember. Don't talk in the fields. Cover your faces. Talk later. Get on your knees and pray. Remember. They have parents who have gangrene, blistered open sores and those that coughed their way in to death, so they take advice seriously. They keep their hands above the bed clothes. They talk when

1

they are inside the house, not out. Their lives are dull, and they remember with dumb senses. They train their hands to stay together away from itchy trunks and digits, and clear their throats with whispered words.

It was nineteen sixty five.

There were hazy and loose surveys that were collected together to form small facts, which pieced together their poor lives. Fifteen percent of the population of the UK owned a colour television; seventy percent owned a black and white television. Seventy percent also owned laptops, but the newspapers were already out of date. The economy was an echo of its last failure but tempted in new money. New retail owners could not understand the lack of sales. Their televisions sung in unison, with choreographed flickering pictures, illuminating the pavement outside, to advertise their availability. Everyone must buy one; they were the latest thing. They were new. The owners hadn't yet noticed the video that controlled the telly never really changed that much.

The population stared blankly at the TV shops and returned expressionless to their homes, where they plugged in their hidden computers. The laptops were just as useless, and a repeated loop of internet pages, but it didn't seem that way. The eyes flickered over the mass of information, and then it is forgetfulness as a few words are found that they need to make them feel that all was usual. It takes a little time to realise that the words don't change, year after year.

Come into my web, said the spider to the fly. The flies were the cold and hungry people of the nineteen thirties, warmed in black wool coats and holding clear plastic umbrellas. The umbrellas are fly wings, in mid-flight. The rain veins them.

The web is shiny, delicate and inviting.

2

There are a million web sites to look through that never change.

The spiders collected details, for later. No one knows who made the web- who the spiders were- they are presumed as dead and dismantled buildings, shrunk yearly to fit in with a fast moving technology, until they become able to fit in to someone's hand.

The human flies were bait as chat bots are fed their chat room banter to repeat and entice.

They are immortalised forever, in a string command.

They are the voice of temptation, as a sub routine.

The computer users are wrapped in sheets of cold silk, on the web, and on the bed, as viruses take them both over.

The News was synchronised, so the edges of both worlds become blurred. The words slipped and dived in conversations, disguised as each other, to fool those that didn't know about computers. Secrecy sold, and there was a lot of money invested in the dead industry. Sixty percent of the population had suffered severe losses because of the storms, the web page announced. That had been true, then.

The hurricanes had started with deep winds, sickly sunshine and public airplanes. The planes had been masked by coal fire smoke and had loud colours with pushy advertising. They had screamed at wild birds while boiling Antarctic ice clouds. They bought nothing with them that was needed. They were the unwanted, carrying the unwanted. They were filled with the pompous and the pick pockets. As the air ships grew in number the sky began to shatter and the seas began to be filled with shit.

The boundaries the planes had left had no clouds to melt away. They had flown the equator, for years, blistering nothing but cheap paint. The air there was still hefty and strong. There

3

were old maps that showed the invisible lines of Cancer and Capricorn, either side of the equator, marking the boundaries where the planes could fly without damaging the atmosphere. The air planes had circled the equator, making the air there like the rings of Saturn, as they gently farted their way past the continents, swapping people and perishables. Over the United Kingdom the fragile cold air steamed and stung as the air planes were allowed to blast their way through. The clouds disappeared into condensation. The atmosphere above the Arctic was already pierced and scarred by satellites. Years before the spy satellites had taken their positions in the sky, anchored with electrical waves and disguised as star systems, and had caused tremors and traumas.

No one really noticed, at first. They had been too enchanted by the magic of aerodynamics and aerial views to see anything else. They were enthralled by the sight of the earth whole, seen for the first time. The world population ate, read, and dreamt the new Atlas as it was shoved into every media. It dominated as it was slipped into every sense. Paintings, books, dance and films alluded to parts of it, in similes and stories; the shape of the world was a horse; the shape of the world was a tea party. The world was shaped as a woman, and the world was shaped as a man. The world was shaped as animals and it was shaped by ague that grew into an argument between land and sea. People talked in allegories and illusions and the shape of the world was sunk into the subconscious, forever and for always, while history was forgotten, and re written to fit. It was the map of the world that they were shown that warped their memories. A little adjusting here and there and the Atlas was a propaganda plaything, a powerful weapon to unite or divide the populace, and a hypnotising spell.

4

It is a feast of a fantasy coming true when cheap electronics followed the sight of the sphere. Electronics flooding the people as water flooded the electronics and the people. There are microwave ovens, video players, remote control, and wifi for sale. Computers and spy watches. They are all vomiting from the stomach of the factories, all at once, in a mish-mash of association with each other. Cd players, mini walkmans, and mp3 players make the eyes grab at them all. It is Halloween, and everyone is being given tricks and treats. The pumpkin is the world, lit up and equipped with eyes.

They are bribes and presents to forget the negatives of the sky scraping sounds.

Then it is all eyes to the skies.

It is now the fault of the populace, not the companies, that the air has split and turned. There are hurricanes, it is implied, because of their disobedience and slovenliness. They did not recycle as they had before, after being told not to recycle. They use too much electricity after being told to. Look, the oil runs dry in their greed. Miners were killed in their search for the coal that they burnt in whimsical need for another plug in the sockets.

See what they have done to the cloudy stratosphere.

The public, as one, had dragged their aching necks up from maps and mobiles, and had obediently looked up. The sky had warped and winded while no one was looking. The airplane lights were shooting stars and the engines were a long drawn out cough that polluted lungs. Swarms started to fly lower.

The night sky star systems were new, but old, weaved the lies the world government told to the enemy, which was themselves. They papered out their peppered propaganda, in time to the tongue twister tornadoes.

The satellites were absorbed into the fables of the horoscope and Greek myths, twisting their way over mythological star crabs and unicorns, to fit in as an extra tale and tail.

These stories, in turn, had been invented to follow the edges of the land, as a distant dot-to-dot. Ireland was a crab, goat, fish or scale, and Norway, Sweden, was the arm of the scales of Gemini. The Greek myth images were cloud formations overlaid on to the stars of the night sky. Night makes day, and day makes night.

The new sky that they had announced was just another few dots in the sky. .

The Orion star system was studied the most. Orion was a connect-the-dots squared egg timer shaped constellation that the media had thrown in to the past, with such force, that it had roused interest for being modern. Also, its pattern had appeared, or had always had been, on pale or ruddy skins in the shape of moles; on arms, legs or torsos. People began to check each other for extra freckles as they used to check for body lice. Babies were watched carefully for signs of stardom and syphilis. They imagined the dots in front of their eyes with a hysterical sight. When the aerials swung in the wind, and the TV was fuzzed; more dots in front of the eyes.

The afflicted were Atlas, carrying the weight of the heavens on their backs, on their arms and on their legs.

But was also the ring worm body bacterium creating its own universe, in negative - the stars were dirt coloured moles instead of bright. Their minute particles would spontaneously combust in a microscopic supernova clothed in warty freckles, and they would be told they had cancer, if any extra moles were found. It would be because, in small, confused logic, the new mole that had just appeared would have been too close to the sun because the new satellite in the sky would have been,

6

said the amateur doctors, who were also amateur astronomers. The rocket would have been burnt out by the engine fire meeting nitrogen. Signals transmitting from it, if it survived, would have been wiped out by the suns radiation, the fake doctors tried to explain, by using their patients as voodoo doll messengers.

The body did echo, so it could be true. The skin may be imitating the earth's atmosphere with erupting moles playing the part of planes, and the poisoned skin below, the part of pollution.

Acne could be the Milky way.

There were still people alive that had blue veins running and pulsating around their body, who had formed in the womb as the world discovered fused plugs. The first covered wires, coiled blue with a yellow stripe, were remembered forever in a veiny sweat. The same fake doctors had diagnosed them as rheumy, pronounced 'roomy'.

It was a joke. They wrapped bandages around a healthy arm to show they had a twisted sense of humerus. The people whose skin was so thin that the veins showed through as blue streaks were given coloured pills to make the veins the correct colour. Blue and yellow make green, green and red make brown. The pills were a deep pink and yellow, to produce a paler tan colour. It was an artist's solution to correct pain, because the doctors were con artists. Rheumy and cancerous. 'Cancerous' is slowed down into separate syllables and mispronounced, so it is 'Canned her, us.' Their doctor lives were a shortened confessional text message, which mingled unnoticed with genuine cases of the same diseases.

The body also told secrets that only the air and government knew, some thought. The people whose skin echoed were, to the rest of the population, the diseased and the gods, bacterial and geniuses. They had existed for centuries, riding on the opinions of the masses, as they imitated the latest thing. Now, in the hurricane sweat of hysterical fever, they were held up as prophets again and seen as past warnings against electrified airwaves; they were being pummelled by sound, they said. The Orion mark was a sign of in-fared babies, of bouncing air, trapped in a place that it couldn't escape. They argued about the appearance of the moles; silent and minute noise was evoluting germs and vibrating genes, to make mounds and moulds; it was traitorous skin which showed the intent of government lab betrayal or it was natural evolution; the star dotted skin was to fool the x-ray eyes of robots and machines, to make the calculations of distance and appearance wrong, when seen on computerised mathematic web cameras.

*

The ring worm riddles toes. It creeps into toe nails, giving them a corrugated appearance. The emergency farm workers stand on plastic shed roofs when they are standing on the ground. The Orion dotted people will pull themselves up to their roof toes by crawling along the ground, army style and grabbing hold of infected feet. They hope their moles will disorientate anything android, as they heard they should, by making the machine misjudge the ground as the sky, in a negative frozen image.

Too much work, too young, will give them a hoofed foot too, as Athletes foot tries to split the foot into horn.

This is what they think of, when they think of the past. They think the devil was born from a wing of fairly mushed wombs. A little earlier in time, a little hotter in the day, and a little colder at night, hooves would have grown, they are sure of it. Their legs would have been covered in thick black hairs as they galloped over house tops, their feet still in the disguise as a row of tatty outhouses, as they jumped over gardens. Ugly feet are a manifestation of a wish, they think. They needed to leap broken buildings and swollen rivers, as the weather poured down pestilence and power lines, and there they were, stuck with bad toes instead, that looked the part of the far away. Be careful of what you wish for, say the Fairee tales, as the weevil might hear and fulfil your yearnings in the least expected ways. They used the dated laptops to warm their feet.

*

The internet spiders had let the mechanical plane flies take over. They had buzzed, in bright bluebottle colours and horse fly formation as they jumbo jetted through global ice. The health warnings, stapled and gathering dust, and hidden in persecuted places, recorded the ill effects of an overdose of them: too many planes, flying at the same time would cause universal major damage in the form of flooding, landslides, earthquakes and extinctions. Tsunamis and hurricanes to swirl the sewers had been predicted, and did happen, as holiday makers packed skis and suntan lotion. The UK, always precariously balanced, as if it were an earthquake edge, already cornered and sliding into the sea, already surrounded by wild weather and sinking beaches, became worse. The weather attacked overnight, and the islands shrunk in fright and floods. The rest of the world suffered a mass of disasters in a domino effect. As the seas swelled, oil platforms tipped. As the oil platforms tipped they polluted the water. As the water became polluted, droughts occurred. Droughts caused famine and breaking earth. The dead polluted the water and the water polluted the animals. The animals died en masse, and polluted the water, and bought the pestilence. The pestilence bought disease, which poisoned those that hadn't drunk the poisoned water. The scorching sun boiled petrol, causing engine fires,

9

and chaos with car crashes. The disasters were all mixed up in a gory weather pattern of extreme heat waves and wind, tipping houses and towers.

When e-coli sprung through taps and leaks of the homes that survived, it turned floors and walls a slippery green and blue. It would turn black eventually, as if the rooms had been slowly beaten and left bruised. The leaking water had been contaminated by the weather, and the water supplies were turned off while damages were repaired. The stunted electricity supply left the mould to develop, photo like, in bouts of darkness.

It was another broken arm, twisted humerus decision to make a feature film out of the crisis's, which made everyone silently panic. The colourful and stark film contrasted sharply against sepia wallpaper and grey smoke-stained furniture. It was too vivid and shocking to eyes used to censored, gentle viewing and musical romances. Viewers recoiled from it and a government they did not recognise. It was broadcast at the cinema, with the wind ripping roofs off outside.

*

Go to church and sing loud.

The walls are as thick as the winds. They were built centuries ago to keep out the wind and the wind swept. Sing loud. Don't scare the children else they will always be scared, forever frozen in copy cat impersonation, unable to help you in your old age. Raise your voices, and hope that someone can hear through the darkness, and send help, but smile while you do it, to hide your own shocked eyes. Singing sounds better than screaming, and it will tempt heroes to pause and listen. The impromptu choir will be the sirens for them, to guide them out of worse danger, and towards other Chrystians. The singing will not alarm them, but alert them.

There are too many dead heroes and lively cowards this century. The brave had died in waves of war and many were frightened by the thought of the sight of them, long dead and unearthed by the weather, swamping the graveyards, coming to rescue them again. The thought gave their voices a quiver; an operatic echo to their song.

The grave yards that had flooded were attached to new modern churches that hadn't been given planning permission. Geology was important when considering the weight and volume of a pile of bones compared to the volume of the UK, which was tipped ridges of mountains. The south-east was sunk, and the stony moor lands were remnants of acidic volcanoes. The deep permafrost that had held it all together had been penetrated by the heat and was melting. Pipes cracked and the earth moved. England's buildings were a calculated house of cards balancing on dry chalk, that hadn't allowed for extra people or buildings.

The old churches had centuries of dead bodies beneath them, turning to gelatine, through pressure and internal heat. It had been planned that the congealing bones would hold the foundations in place, should the worse happen. It had been a century's long joke that the earth would fall away, revealing hair brush bristles of enormous proportions made from the mass of coffins that had been carefully interred on top of one another. It was the dead that helped the living, that helped the world bond itself, so it didn't fall apart when the ice receded; the dead of the people, of birds, animals, insects and plants all clinging into rough glue to stop the land from sinking. The very old hadn't believed in cremation, they believed in recycling.

While England was still fracturing in the corner of Europe, unreachable by friends, the newspapers sunk into a frenzy of power. They printed that the UK had political differences with

11

the EEC when Europe couldn't reach the UK because of the weather. As the weather got worse the newspapers declared that England was also separate from Wales and Scotland. They printed political divides and angry disputes rather than the truth; that Wales and Scotland couldn't be reached either. Then there was a north and south divide in England as roads broke up and flooded. Emergency vehicles only, but the reports suggested religious differences. The newspapers had gone mad. When they run out of land to divide, they began to divide man and woman, parents and children, with stories of battles of the sexes and of age, and colour. It was if they were slicing and dicing the population.

The reporters had been replaced by criminals who had swooped in on a two week sight seeing trip, some said, in horrified hushed tones. They were chopping society up, and burning bridges, to keep themselves fed and warm.

Others thought it was the language of the eyes that had caused the chaos. When the mimes had told each other they were going to get rid of their black and white television set, that they didn't like black and white anymore, racism was born, and repeated, until it became fact.

'Colour tv ', in their silent world, was misinterpreted as 'our law, me.' The riots start with friend talking to friend about the latest gadget, without opening their mouths, and one accusing the other of bullying. When they get rid of the colour television in favour of an LCD screen, they look as if they are overthrowing the government in favour of a seedy world. The camera records, not just two people, but thousands of them, all looking as if they are secretly, silently plotting, and sends in the riot police, followed by the army, to deal with the civil uprising, that has been planned, it seems, to occur with the bad weather. No one thinks that the remote radio frequencies, used by the mobile technology have contributed to the heated, warped air; the connection stays with the airplanes and factory pollution.

The explanation of misinterpretation seemed more probable, more acceptable, than mad newspaper reporters.

It is accidental war.

*

The Chrystians wet the baby's head in the font. They were scientific, not spiritual. They had seen the map of the world a long time before it was published and it was their history, their science, and the root of their belief. They hid in stern buildings and had humane thoughts. They believed in the transfiguration of the world. A world created by mathematical reflections, refractions and angles. Cos, Sin, Tan. Calculus. That people are the earth's membrane photos of the sky and land masses. Jaesus, for them, is a name for those chemicals that make the cells change to human ones, with splendid heat and chilled awareness of the universe. It is a bacterial bio chemical that exists in the highest air, so tiny and minute, it hides under the microscope. Jaesus takes a fuzzy photo of the distant shapes and the heavens rain it down within the holey water.

'Where do you come from? And where did your parents come from?' asked the doctors' surveys as they inspected moles and prominent features. They wanted to see what water was drunk because the swallowed water is water that has seen the world, or part of it; they wanted to know the angle of light that had penetrated it and what part of the alphabet of watery building blocks it had hidden within its chemical folds. It is a haemoglobin hemisphere. The world atlas is all and everything, and they think it is contained in a drop of water.

13

The shapes of the UK coastlines are very important to them. England is an x ray of a pregnant woman's pelvic bone, when it is seen from the direction of Scotland.

There is a baby that is Ireland.

To them, this is the root of humanity, and the reason humanity exists. They are the photograph that was handed back to the beast to make human.

Some also think that the UK's image was reflected by the icy sky into the sea, where the image was caught in minute sea cells, and blown across the land in windy blasts that transformed the living, as they breathed in the air, into human form. We come from the sea, they theorised, and played with crystals and water.

Another view of the transfiguration was from the god believers, who thought that the image of the UK, and the other countries, had been reflected outwards, into space, to make a supreme being. The supreme being had lent the embryo the vision back, in telepathic generosity, so that the baby could become the same form.

It was still all angles and logarithms that made up their separate thoughts though, and bonded them. They were all mathematicians, with a mathematicians reasoning and the shape of the UK united them. The land was the foundation of their Chrystian beliefs of transfiguration, their reason for being in the UK; their pilgrimage and their undeniable proof.

*

The font that the baby's head is dipped into is the symbolic pelvic bone and England's coastline. The water joins the baby to the metaphorical placenta, and also to England. The baby is learning about geography and biology while being baptised. It is splashed with water in the church, because it will be the church that the adult will run to when the baby that is Ireland

14

and England is splashed with water, when the adult is feeling as helpless as a baby. There will be no help or hope from anywhere; no one can get to the islands when the weather is bad, besides inland will be having the same mud slide.

Run to church, and be surrounded by family and friends. There will be food from the harvest that has been stored. There will be water from the fountain. There will be protection from pestilence and disease.

The baby is held to the heavens, as the sun shines through the stained glass and the singing begins. It is the United Kingdom and Eire that shapes the living embryo with a skull and fashions it with eyes too, according to the world of transfiguration. This is because when the islands are seen from the direction of the rising sun, they look like eyes and nose; skull like in their appearance. The picture has changed, and the embryo changes with it. The stained glass is a simile of the rainbow of chemicals that the atmosphere and sun creates, of the changeable layers it contains, and how they fashion in to form.

The baby is dressed in white netting, to trap any mosquitoes or water fleas. It is longer than the baby needs. It is a persuasion for the baby, to grow into it, to grow taller and stronger.

When the ceremony is over, the white smock and bonnet are checked for blood stains, left by bloated tics and squashed fleas. It happens so quickly, but they can time and position the insect, so it doesn't happen again. They will gently shuffle along, and leave a space for the nit to fly into. It is their joke about the regularity of life. They will use the grown-out-of long smocks on the fields, to protect the face against the cut corn and flying dust. It will be used turban like, just like it was in the past, wrapped around the mouth, nose and ears to protect them from a scabby invasion. It is entwined with the hair to stop the cloth blowing away in the high winds.

The oldest field clothes they wear are stained a bitty yellow in places, and the adolescent workers are awed anew at the unmovable paisley pattern that the crop fields generate. Clothes are mostly boiled, and left a grimy white from the bacteria killing bleach that is added to the water, so this sign of the forgotten is momentarily interesting.

The christening is made a ceremony and an occasion to remember, so the baby doesn't forget or lose itself in the memories of another, similar person. The baby is given its Chrystian scientists' name, the one that isn't written. A secret name, which is proof of identity to their closest blood relatives, and a name an impostor wouldn't know. It seems paranoid, but it isn't. Safety is in numbers that cannot be infiltrated.

*

There is, in the room the emergency farmers change in, a mountain of dead scrawny insects that have been shaken from sweaty work clothes. They have been swept hazardously, by broom and hazy breezes, in to corners that trail off into lines of the room. Their trails are reminiscent of forgotten italic font and pubic hair. They are a dirty story, shaken out from a blown about porn magazine, and as unchanging as one.

The workers do not notice. The sight is just out of the peripheral of their conjunctivitis ridden eyes. They look like lumpy-eyed Chinese.

*

The public swimming pool stays open, for hygiene reasons. People are squashed in. The women have bouffant, aristocrat type hairstyles, fashioned that way in the hope that if the worse was to happen they will metamorphosis into life saving equipment. They have shelf heads and bloated breasts. The

16

fashion is again everywhere. The dimness is recreated, echoed, in the media, and big breasts become more fashionable for their word association. The women bob around the swimming pool, hoping someone will cling on to their buoy like tits or hair, to validate their helpfulness. They have nautical disinfected swimming costumes, bad taste and white lipstick.

In contrast, there are over dressed stinking dark crooks that boil swans outside, at the scenic park, observed by the swimmers through the open, glassed wall. Their features and bodies are obscured by all-over black cloaks. They cook part of the swan in a caked black saucepan, over a one ring calor gas stove, and collect weeds from the well kept garden beds to flavour it.

Before the glass wall's door can be locked, they tend to wade in, fully dressed, scaring the already frightened with broken teeth and pincer, inquisitive hands that are used to searching for hidden pockets. They had been taught to grab and to handle other people as if they were cheap, stolen objects, and they bully themselves a space. Their attitude shows a wiliness to hurt and annoy. If they are brushed off, they will begin to argue that they are seen as non-human like; a black flea or beast. If others do not move out of the way for them, they are similarly accused of being offensive rather than defensive.

The glass door is not the entrance and they haven't paid, it was left open because of the heat wave, explains an attendant, over and over again.

They have to be told every time they use the glass door. It is obvious that they are the same people each time, but they are blind to their own deceit, when others can see it clearly.

The group talk in a mixture of an unknown language and a scouse English accent, calling and beckoning others like them from the park outside. The amount and size of the acquaintances vary. The police and social services are regularly called as the   group continually refuse to pay for entrance, and there is nearly always a struggle. Some of them wear long black wigs over afro haircuts, which they let fall into the chlorinated water. It is a distraction which is hypnotising in its regularity. The wigs are left to float through a babbling brook of bums before being grabbed and thrown out at walls. Rat like, they are too alike to the floods to be amusing, and they are left, like the dark corners of the emergency showers.

The swimming pool also has a scattering of insulting afro haircuts, grown extra long every time an outbreak of hair nits is announced in the local paper. They place themselves around the swimming pool in a recognisable pattern that insects use.

They wait to be told that they cause offence. They want control over people. To gain control they put their words into another's mouth and paint themselves as victims when they are the aggressors. They think control is power, and power is money. They hope to raise millions by being minions for their loose cult, and they often freeze with empathy at the ejection of those that are like minded.

The wigs are discreetly, eventually, rescued by them, seen only by the hidden CCTV camera and a few bathers.

As the country fills up with stagnant water, the sea side residents move inland, using surviving holiday caravans as temporary accommodation. They flock to the public swimming pools too, to wash in, and the overworked cleaners overlook the hardened toothpaste stains in favour of cleaning the darkening patches of mould in the shower cubicles. There is a foot bath and showers to use before entering the swimming pool, to decrease the risk of infection, but the foot bath is forgotten in the cleaning schedule as the stuffed toilets flood diarrhoea. There are uncontrollable outbreaks of verrucas and warts mixed with vomiting stomachs, and people are urged to wash their hands after swimming.

*

And Jaesus leaves a trail of flowers.

Let us pray. On your knees. Let me see the soles of your feet, and see if they have been flowered. Press your hands together. Can you feel the infection of warts in them? They feel like the coins of a fairy, and look like miniature anuses.

Orion is in the sole, as veruccas. Now they walk the heavens and stand on the clouds, watching a mini hurricane at a distance as the swirling water leaves the swimming pool footbath through the plug hole. They are gods.

The new infectious outbreaks make good CCTV though. The shocked consumers are held in a dreamlike hysteria as they talk without speaking. Their children blow bottle bubbles at each other as a sign of acknowledgement, lessening the stigmata of infection with soft playful games, watching as the bubbles pop and leave sud rings on everything. They are cleaning the air with soap. The air will become as sterile as the moon, and humans landed on the moon while the moon landed on their feet, as tiny pictures and as craters. They are all yeast ridden, and blowing bubbles inside out, and watching them pop on the surface of the skin. They are becoming the rising bread and bubbling wine with the fermenting infections. They stagger on their infected feet, and belch after eating, as if they have had too much of both, when they have had neither. There is a shortage of bread and wine, and most rely on allotments or local farmers for food. Some pick wild fruit, but when the fruit and flowers of the wild are eaten, they are populated with their own tiny eco system of infection, that lay eggs in the bladder and poisons the intestines.

19

When it is hurricane weather, the infections are blown in with the wind though, whether or not there is wild fruit in the fruit bowl.

Shut the windows before the high winds gain strength and the swarms are forced lower. There are masses of the things everywhere, each carrying a Jaesus coin to burn into everything.

Hide and clean, like your parents did. Don't touch each other. Dry your clothes inside the house. Don't use public utilities. Wash fruit before eating. They will burn your gullet otherwise, as they catalyse.

The diseased masses look to the sky and worry silently that the ring worm, verrucas and warts look more familiar to it than they used to be, as if they weren't an ailment listed, but a morphing simile that is really caused by the satellite dishes and infra-red. The warnings of radiation sickness from the eighteen hundreds are remembered with forbearing and the real doctors whisper among themselves, while rummaging through old medical books.

The internet isn't working, and the analogue aerials are blown away, stabbing the air in artistic interpretation of the starvation of the country. The picture on the television, when it works, is another bitty piece of living art as it hazily broadcasts, looking like a window covered in buzzing black ants.

When the television works it shocks then soothes, showing flash frames of unobtainable consumables in between live repeated footage of disasters and self mocking comedians. It exploits the hunger for news of loved ones with substitute replacements that are safe and well and in front of a live audience.

When it is announced that all the livestock in the United Kingdom – chickens, cows, sheep, goats and horses – have become infected with diseases and are inedible, the country thinks it has been rewound. It is the war years again, with queues and black-markets. The countryside becomes forbidden and meningitis ridden. There are hints of Sweeny Todd pies and burgers, so new take-aways stay empty while would-be customers wonder why the corner shops have suddenly, seemingly changed ownership.

It has all happened within a couple of months.

It is a roller-coaster of death and destruction. It is an invasion of criminals disguised as illegal immigrants, and illegal immigrants invading as refugees.

Then there are the zealous map readers, who have come because of the other shape of the UK. They have come because they have turned the map around, and are looking from the west so that baby Ireland lies on a bed of straw that is England and Scotland, instead of the pelvic bone. They are witnessing the birth of Chryst, they think. It is the baby Jaesus in his manger, surrounded by the other countries as animals, that they are looking at as they arrive via Europe. They land into chaos and with a glazed spiritual look, joining anyone that looks the same stunned.

It is all too much for many of the people; the weather, the overload of stationary information that the internet gives, and the strangers that gesture with unknown meanings.

When people looked into each others eyes, there is no life left, just a dim awareness of their surroundings. It is a lost world in the confused cities. Groups form and reform as people wander without cause, echoing the loose friendships that they have seen, play-acted, on the TV. They have a common bond in television viewing, they imply, so can't be all bad. Old cults greedily recruit the lost and new in a practised swoop. New cults are born and formed, bonded while the people are stupid with the loss of lost loved ones.

*

Let use pray.

The sermons are written to be repeated, in a monotonous drawl.

They are full of love, to combat the hatred, and the most basic of emotions. They are aimed to be stronger in their constancy than the behaviour of the weather and of the criminals.

And then the priest raises himself up in front of the congregation and the words from the bible are nonsense. The parables are strewn with urges of endearment, familiarity and a smattering of knowledge. Incomprehensible verses that are contrived to slow the mind, before the money bowl is passed around to be filled with what the congregation cannot afford. The congregation are there to learn how to ignore those that they can't understand, that bully them for coins and pounds, who won't help in saving another, but pretend to be their closest friend.

When the bowl is passed back empty, the cults are not in control, and the priest has earned his wage.

Chapter 2

The swimming pool is a place for swimming and sometimes sex. The sex is on the direction of the television. It hypnotises with images of stripped women, and muscled men. There is sex in the baths, and on the beaches. Seaside holiday romances when there are no seaside resorts or romances left. It is because it is clean water that the images entice. Clean water sterilises the genitals, so the babies produced will be as clean as the TV stars. Clean is healthy, and healthy is rich. Everyone wants to be rich. It is also important, is the undertone, that the population replenishes itself. There is, in the future, planes to fill and supermarket items to be sold. The swimming pool people wear the chlorinated water like perfume, to advertise their sexiness and hygiene. The hairstyles are still bobbing there, on skinny legs, not yet fattened by the laziness of car use.

A sauna and Jacuzzi has been built where the handicapped entrance had been. Avoided by those that were suspicious of money being spent when everywhere was poverty, it was mostly used by prostitutes and the staff.

And the wind raged outside and the drinking water was rationed.

*

She thinks she was conceived in the aftermath of a swimming session. Her mother, she supposed, had smelt of bleached water.

Her father had probably cleaned his skin by sauna and steam. He would have been too wary to use the pool, because of the risk of infecting others with his skin condition. He would have smelt of hot oils.

His skin had ulcers. Not many ulcers, just one, but it was the size of plenty. The ulcer stripped away the top layer of skin off his ankle, every July, leaving a red, perfectly round, raw skinless blister. It was the size of a small plate and sat on his shin, curdling around the edges. When it appeared he limped. If he was made to exercise it, a line of bloody creases would appear from the centre, branching out like a red spider.

At a guess, the sauna had been empty. Her father, though probably not shy, and on friendly speaking terms with the prostitutes, would have avoided them when he needed to. He would have sat on the bench, waiting, leg outstretched.

Passing children, afflicted with a combination of the holey names would have stopped to sympathise, or would have given him a knowing look when faced with a sore of such gigantic proportions, within their eye level.

Her father was about forty when she had been conceived. He had sky blue eyes and blonde grey brows. His teeth had been mostly lost through a thin diet that lasted through the Second World War, and only his lower set of teeth remained intact. They had grown in to place wobbly and crossed.

The fashion was for teeth as straight as tomb stones, as if they were a brittle toe nail under a magnifying glass, so his false upper set were set with a regularity that didn't match his features. He wasn't a natural foot mouth- a foot mouth was big enough to show twelve teeth in one smile, and was sarcastically full of sole, or soul - he was smaller jawed.

Despite his lack of nutritional diet, he was well built, and tall.

There was a sticker on the changing room wall that read 'please do not wear contact lenses or false teeth beyond this sign' and her father would have taken them out of his mouth at the last moment, keeping them in his trunk pocket. Teeth had been expensive, and sold well on the black market.

25

Most of the thieves were gypsy children. They darted in and out of the changing rooms with a pretext of playing, giggling at each other while silently signalling another target.

Her mother may have kept away from him, mistakenly thinking that she would be seen as one of the swimming pool prostitutes if she went too near the sauna, which she never could have been. They never changed their appearance or age, and, ironically, looked less oily than her mother.

She would have swum near the changing rooms instead, equally aware of the thieves, to whom she regarded with fascination, lust and distrust. They were Peter Pans lost boys, whom could be of either sex. They were also the water babies that lived at the bottom of the pool, travelling from their home in the Thames in a swell of flood water, to find new sunken treasure in the shores of other counties. They were an unwanted but fascinating novelty event, scary and criminal.

The visit to the swimming pool would have been quick. It was too busy, but cheaper than boiling drought water for a bath.

*

It is in the first few days of conception the genetics are set.

'Rubble bubbles, boils and troubles, add the wing of a bat, the tongue of a frog and stir in the eye of a ghost. Add pepper to taste, and sea salt to see. Adieu. You now have you, instead of me." The children's rhyme is in a children's book. On the cover is a cauldron and three dark witches, clothed in black crayon. They have tall pointed hats and misshapen noses. The dead animals are added to the cauldron water, and the water is never boiled. It is just warmed, as the temperature for yeast is warmed. It is the optimum temperature for bacteria, and the bubbles in the cauldron are gases from the dead animals, decomposing. The cauldron is as a metaphor for the heat-waved rivers, and their germy mixtures. The witches are all the continents, darkened by dismal cloud and turned upside down, to make a recognisable picture of a coven.

The body heat of her mother would have been variable, but about the same as the cauldron. She would have been full of suppressed fever and cheap Babycham.

Her mothers' grandmother had been born in England. Her mother had storm-weathered blood with a natural hint of malaria and typhoid, because of this. The weather was jumping from blistering heat to tropical downpours, and hinted at the same diseases becoming the norm.

She supposes that her one day old self struggled for identification, and a sign to what she would eventually become as the worlds of the sperm and egg met, and as it decided on the most useful trait of them both. Her father, steamed and stifled, would have limped to the pub after his sauna and cooled himself with an apple cider, buying the Babycham to take home with him. Supermarkets didn't really exist. The shops were closed early evening and weren't open on a Wednesday or a Sunday. Her father worked the same hours, and Sundays was a church day.

Wednesday's child was full of Woe, or toe. She may have feet teeth instead of her dad, and be full of swole that will turn into soul.

He would have bought her mother ten cigarettes. The nicotine, breathed in through pursed lips and stare shaped eyes, stifled some of the oxygen in the blood, and hormones, trained to react in conjunction with expected bad news, would have flooded her mothers system at regular times.

There may have been a power cut during her conception. Both of her parents would have shared a split second admission of fright in an intimate wide eyed exchange, while they held onto each other in the dark. The adrenaline, which had been conserved for the nightly news that didn't happen, would have flooded their bodies. The heavy, invisible, poisoned air would have been exchanged in the lungs and tedious flies waved away with an exasperated sigh as her mother smoked and blew air at them. Her mother had learnt to do that from the cinema.

A sip of the contaminated water in the morning, and her embryo self's fate was sealed. The chromids split and doubled in confused wonderment of the excited and energetic blood it was receiving.

Her mother wasn't a Hairstyle. Her hair was too flat and her breasts to small. Her figure was turd like in its shape, and her fat squashed breasts looked more like a bum sitting on top of it. The bra was a girdle at both ends. She was cellulite with fatty loose tissue, and her stomach rolled and spread with no muscle to hold it in shape. The baby, herself, sat unnoticed under loose nylon flares. Her mother, anaesthetised against the world with alcohol and adrenaline, sat transfixed alternately by the TV and the laptop, as she grew inside her.

When the embryo woke up she knew of her bumpy beginning and of imminent danger. She knows of birth and death, of cells multiplying, of abortion, which she thinks she is experiencing.

*

The first showing of a video of panic footage from New Orleans is being broadcast. It is of a hurricane. It shows dead bodies floating on the surface of drowned streets, and blood soaked victims of knife gangs lying on ambulance beds. It was a hurricane to end all hurricanes, to end all life.

The abortion, if that is what it is, hasn't worked. Her mother didn't go to the hospital because she thought it had been taken over by people who weren't qualified, and had tried a home remedy of gin and aspirin to help her lose the just discovered pregnancy. There was blood, so she was satisfied there wasn't an embryo any more.

But the embryo, herself, is alive. The blood is from her mother's anus. After the gin had been drunk, with the aspirin dissolved in it, she had eaten a curry, which had upset her stomach. To abort her, her mother would have had to have had enough of the drugs to kill herself too.

She falls back to sleep in awkward knowledge of being unwanted, punctuated by television input. Her mother is urged to move while the adverts are filling the screen. It is time for a tea break, it hints. The stomach muscles contract as she rises, alerting the embryo, and in floods the information pumped out by the television. It is pre natal brain control imprinting brand loyalty. She dreams of living long enough to see colours, and to smell clean washing, as her mother moves to the kitchen, to make a cup of tea in the advert break. The advertising is always sunny, warm and clean. The pictures are of sunlight, hot food and hygienic, sweet smelling, stain free clothes, and as the boiled water floods down the oesophagus the combination gives her dreams of laundry, without knowing what it is. The words linger and mingle with the warmth.

She is a Pavlov's dog, conditioned with the hot and cold words, to reach out for a shopping basket. She will buy thermos flasks, blankets and hot tea in trained response, when she is born.

The embryo is in unfeeling pain. It is another automatic feeling as her mother's muscles contract in horror. The muscles squash her as if she is excrement to be pushed out. If she is born, she is told, she will probably be born deformed.

More blood appears in her mother's knickers and her mother decides to go out to celebrate her loss and commiserate with the over-sea weather deaths. It is Babycham and cigarettes as she swaps stories with other people who viewed the site of the devastated football stadium. She will drop out of her mother's womb, in the pub toilet, or into a white plastic bag, to be sold to the animal experimenters or to the butchers. No one will notice that she was ever there, so no one will notice that she has gone. Her skin will be held under the lighted microscope, and will be marvelled at for its healing properties, while she sits and watches parts of herself being tested.

Embryos are sought after for their speedy recoveries in response to trauma. She will split and heal to please the doctors, and they will wear clean clothes to please her. She will not last long, but would have contributed to keeping the wrinkles at bay.

The skin at each side of her eye brows has split open, as if in response to her thoughts. The splits are coin shaped. One instantly begins to heal, as if it is demonstrating the words she has been told, and holds itself together with a slight twist of her body. It is a tiny straw shape while the other blister stays open, with healing skin growing behind it.

She is convolted by another piece of news on the television.

There is E.coli contamination at the hospital. It is not a repeat. The news is local. The hospital has been used to store the dead from the hospital, north of the town, which in turn was used to store the dead from further north.

There is ten in the bed, and the little one is dead, all over, all over. So they all rolled over And one fell out. All over, all over.

It is musical morgue, and when the ambulance siren stops, the dead are shuffled along.

Everyone is stunned, and everything is closed down, including the pub. The overspill of the dead is from the coasts. They have been washed in with tsunami seawater and driftwood.

Her life has been saved.

*

The open sore on her father's leg is big enough for her to dream in. She sees it without seeing it. It is womb like in colour, and large enough to be called one. The ailment had grown in the telling, and the fables named it a whole woman instead. The woman is hanging on to his ankle, slave-like and devoted, in paintings and in films. The woman is slave-like because his leg also looks as if it has been rubbed with a lathe. The words conveniently rhyme.

He cannot walk away, and limps while the woman is there, as he tries to. The woman bleeds for him as he tries to move. It is menstruation as his ankle wrinkles blood in an outline of a womb.

His leg had become an opera, and a drama.

The woman is no longer his dutiful wife but is his mother, as the menstruation creases worsen and becomes a birthing instead. He is Shakespeare's Tempest, and Ariel and Miranda are his leg. He is Macbeth.

And woman was born of man, from his spare rib, because that is what the creases looked like when he finished exercising it. His ankle thinks it is also a sternum, thought the new story tellers, who missed the beginning of the myth. Woman grew from there, and the humps of toes became breasts as she looked down at herself.

Feet are meat, are milk, are food, just the same.

Her father's sore on his ankle is not permanent. When it appears once a year, with its red, rheumy, gummy look, it is always at the same time of day, always on the same day, of the same month. This century it is compared to the planet Mars. The planet Mars is in the newspapers and the television and appears at a regular time too, in its orbit. Mars used to be another moon, according to radio scientists, but time has twisted and warped its name to echo scarring and blemishes.

Mars her fathers leg, and Ma's her father's leg.

The heavens meet the earth, as her father's foot does as he takes a step. The movement of the ankle is a heaving one as muscles pull on other muscles.

It is heaving, it is heaven.

Mars, in the sky, would be the same distance away from the sun, as her father's sore circumference is from its centre, on the ankle bone. They share coincidences and comparisons.

When her fathers sore appears it complements the Orion freckle stars, that are on another's body. He only needs to stand next to some one who has them, and they become a distant thousand or so miles wide and part of the heavenly bodies of the universe. They are space on bodies, rather than bodies in space. It is another part of the world of transfiguration, where the skies are echoed in the skin, even when some of the skies can't be seen. It is cumulus, and integral calculus, as angles float around corners to explain what else could be there, in the sky, by looking at the body. The person is getting the bigger picture. It is a picture of the skies that sit on her father's leg. It is reverse transfiguration. The scientists that believe that the sore is a photo of Mars will hunt for other planets by putting his leg under a microscope. It is a monk's calculus calculation to find a shape in the sky that is in ratio with a scabby appearance on the body. It is theoretic mumbles and a picture of transfiguration, sold on to people who want it to be real. There are other freckles and unknown scratches, they want to believe, as they look through broken telescopes and play with Photoshop, that are planets and stars.

Her father's foot is a bio chemistry industry feast, for biologists, as it eats through the skin. Enzymes and Ph are collected on the pin head, and put under glass, the dead butterfly is flicked away, and forgotten. At this ph, and this heat, the circle will grow this big; as the warmth of syphilis is on the skin, as the gassy sun is to the invisible planet of Mars. It's two moons become the end of an ankle bone, in the darkness.

It is also Jaesus, with a view to the heavens, and a view to the earth, that makes her fathers ulcer. It is the same type of outer reflection that made God, some think, and all at once her father is Gods child on earth. They are miniature and massive twins, in extreme thoughts.

She carries his genes, in miniature. Her pennies from heaving, sitting on her brow, shaped as if she had been prodded already by people with nothing to do, are explained away in shades of temperature.

She sleeps and dreams

*

She names herself Shannon, which is the name of a river that runs through her father's mind and is close to his own birthplace in Ireland. She names herself Emerald because the colour sounds good. The surname that she will share with her father, which will be on her tombstone, begins with 'Mer' which is French for sea. She is the river Shannon that travels through the emerald green to find the Mer, the sea. The knowledge shapes her face, she thinks, and the cartilage in her nose bends as it forms, to allow a simile of Galway to be seen through her nostrils, so that her father's genes can breathe. She knows the map of the world and Ireland is her nose, when the United Kingdom are the eyes. Shannon's face is deformed, but only when compared to perfection, as her genes shape themselves in to a closer observance of her world. One nostril is slightly rounder and one eye is slightly smaller.

As the days pass, and the earth spins, England is seen from another angle and her face changes to fit. England is a pig, and one of the pig's nostrils are higher than the other, on the map, and her nostril is pulled up a little more, to emulate.

Her exact location is pinpointed with a small, white mole, on her forehead, and it doubles as a faraway sun to her two scars that are Mars, that are sitting on her brows.

She is yin yang to her father. Upside down, and distant.

Her eyebrows are the prime meridian in this imagined UK, in it's guise as eyes. The pinpoint is just above one eyebrow, and would be in the south, if she tilted her head to match the map. The hairline on one side is East Anglia. Her hair will become the North Sea and the English Channel. Her ear is Le Mans, in France, but Le Mans is also a beauty mark under her eye.

The silhouette of her face could also become a map of France. She will have to have a side portrait drawn for her, white against black. It will be placed on a family string of portraits. Together her families' faces would make up the world, or a continent, fitting together like a jigsaw puzzle, with their slight deformities and shore line profiles.

Her eyes are yellow brown, green and blue. The blue circles the pupil, and then it is green. The brown is nestling the irises. They are earth, trees, and sky, as her thoughts see them. The centre of the earth is the black irises. One has the silhouette of a baby bird in it, picked out in brown against the green. The brown shoots up, like tree trunks, to make a beak. To make her look more vulnerable, her iris is the baby bird's over-large black eye. It is an exaggeration of her fears. The world is full of robotic creatures, and birds are one type of them. Her face is a bird's eye view of the world, and her eye is a view of a bird who took the photo. The mechanical birds are cameras and spies. They are not stiff, but are as lucid as other birds, and are

34

made of metal and machined feathers. She will show them the mirror image in her eye, should they fly too near, and they will fly away, thinking she is already watched by another machine.

The other pupil is shaped as a pentagram, and is browner in one half. It is the Pentagon, bombed. It is a shell of a building, and an old ruin, already. The eye is old news and is crowded with shadowy skulls. She is scared already of loud noises, and of the news programmes that broadcast the thudding, deafening sounds. The noise makes her shudder and pause in what she is making, which is herself. She doesn't want any more, she already has one. She is shutting the door on the salesman, with a no thank you, don't want to buy anymore reasoning.

Her eyes are her television and internet pictograms; an eye to the sky, and another to the ground. The world talks in pictograms and anagrams. It will understand her eyes, and her fears, when it sees them.

Her blood paints for her, while she sleeps. It is alive.

*

She still sees without seeing.

*

There is a single black hair on her father's blonde eye brow, that stands proud like an antenna. It also looks like a rocket leaving the earth from the boiling yellow sand dunes of his eye lid. It is a rocket, as seen from a distance. The hair appears and disappears, with an internal timing too.

The rocket it impersonated, or simulated, burned the French African sands as it was launched into space. The sands are on the thigh of the horse that the lower continents of the globe make up. The thigh of the horse becomes her fathers' ankle and when the single black hair disappears and the red sore re appears on his leg, it is the rocket launch. It is ratio and rota. His ankle is the ankh of Egypt.

35

'Spare rib' is a slurred pronunciation of 'hair shin' said with a silent mouth and a point with the eyes. The shin belonged to the hair. Her thin, developing, ribs were brow hairs.

*

The DNA of that single black hair was threading through her body. It is a needle, embroidering the skin. There is a line of moles from her head to her toes. They snake through her skin, down her body, leaving knots and bows here and there. The line twists and turns, inside and out, before emerging from her anus in a curved dot-to-dot piggy tale. She has a line of diagonal moles along her chest, like a winners sash or military adornment, which disappear on the hip. It shows the path of the rocket, she thinks.

They, the world, are still talking as if the world map is a farm yard, and her mind talks as if the body was planetary systems, bound together by magnetism and atoms. In the monks' scientists' world, an orbit was bone socket, and the sun was the hormones of the pituitary gland, heating the blood. The planets were the planes of the bone; the long length from one end to the other. The monks would have said that the lump that balanced on her dad's brow, that the single black hair stood upon, was called the mound of Mercury. The mound of Mercury was closest to the sun, the pituitary gland, and disappeared along with the single hair, every year.

The yearly appearance of that single hair, and the yearly scorched ankle was a mystery. No one knew, not really, what it was, why it happened in sequence. It was a common belief that he may have been born too near the Northern lights, which can be seen from England and Ireland in the cold air of November.

It is safer to blame natural events, rather than man or machine. It is easier to come to terms with even though nature is equally confusing, shocking and puzzling as a government, it is less dangerous than one.

Where her mother and father live the Aurora Borealis appears in the sky only once a year, on a regular day, and in a shade of red. It is not the colour that is surprising, but the shape and rhythm of its appearance, with timing just like her father's ailments. It is shaped like the smoky start of a genie, or the smudged outline of an equilateral triangle balancing on one point. The sight of the aurora was, in Georgian custom, portrayed as the tail end of a Father Christmas. He wore a dinner jacket in this myth, and the tail end dipped in the air over England. When he was turned upside down, the aurora became his sleep hat. He is head first down the chimney, out of the darkness and into the light. He was trapped within the square of the fire place, which looked like a television surround.

There is a cult to whom this event is the most important thing to have ever happened.

They call themselves the 'Horis'

Horis, air is, pore is, whore is, auroras. They are chain letter people; fake London cockneys, that rhyme everything – words, actions, things and happenings. It is a sing-song karaoke cult.

The aurora appears regularly on the fourteenth of November, every year, unless it snows, at four pm.

They have played with the numbers.

That is 11. 14.4 = 12 X 12. Twelve and twelve are the hours in the day and night, and the amount of months in a year, before it appears again. Eleven is the number before twelve.

Time is an intricate puzzle of numbers for them.

The womb is the aurora, they think. It is the same shape, and the menstruation appears just as punctually between the legs as the aurora does in the sky. It is a one to twelve ratio. 1:12. It is another part of the number puzzle.

Just as her father is named the son of god, by some, they name the women of their cult 'Goddesses'. Women contain the universe, because they contain the aurora. They are, they say, the chosen ones. The men are born of the goddesses, so therefore are gods themselves. It is a cult of self worship and self delusion. They slow down time, they claim, by using words and setting scenes.

They count with aurora timing; one yearly menstruation in the sky is one month. That makes a twelve year old, a one year old. When a person is twenty four years old they are two years old.

The Horis claim to have invented time, the watch, the clock, and the calendar, with their observant calculations. The woman's menstruation is the minute hand of the watch, and the Aurora is the hour hand of the watch. 'Hour' is 'aurora', said with speed.

It makes sense to count like that, they think, in lands that are cradling a baby who never grows old.

The cult is young. They invented themselves in the mid eighteen hundreds, and are still awed by their connections.

The time-keeping kept the members of the cult young and innocent; gullible. They are malleable and managed. The members of the cult are told to pretend to be spell bound and blind to their own age to persuade others to be. It is part of the cult's big plan to take over the world by stopping time, by showing the same time and actions repeatedly, with no detection of the people making the actions changing. They will swap the original inventor for a Horis dummy one, with everyone watching. Their victim will seem to grow old, then young again, as they are swapped with some one less knowledgeable, but who looks the same. The cult thinks they are convincing, by being convinced. They have been persuaded that there are no lines on their faces and no lies in their mouths. They want others to believe they hold the key to eternity.

The cult's gods and goddesses do no work themselves, because they are gods and goddesses. If they strain their arm or brain, they may alter the night sky or the alignments of planets. This, they say, would cause earthquakes and death. They are entitled to do nothing and take credit. The Chrystian god does the same. They have a smattering of Chrystian transfiguration in their thoughts, and an echo of her fathers ailments to support their claims. He has a week off work every year, because of the ulcer.

They have the excuse of someone else's religion for every criminal act.

The Horis is also 'horsi'. They mis-spelt their cult name on purpose when the shape of the world was revealed, and they saw that the resemblance of continents were similar to the shape of a horse. They are the baby that is sliding off the nose of the horse, but aim to take over the world, by swinging themselves around, pendulum like, to ride it, and train it to obey. Ireland was their mascot. They will always be innocent and baby like, as they take over, as they count in Horis years. They will be every ones baby and will never be old enough to speak. They will impersonate others, and be whore see, whore do instead, and never need to learn other languages.

They will be trained to copy, but not be able to learn.

They are whores, because the 'w' at the front of their name shows the continents they will imitate. They are told they will be as cold as the ice of Greenland, but hot as Africa, when they meet the middle, which is a Chinese tea time. Their eyes will always smile, while inside they will be fuming, like the hidden volcanoes of the same land, as they meet their twin.

The whores sell their own flesh, before selling others. They are moonies, monsters and pie makers, as they prostitute their children or other peoples.

They are moronically acting out the illegal selling of the UK and Ireland, they claim, as they invite strangers inside their most religious and best kept secret, their aurora womb, as they lead them under the red light. They have been taught to be intimate with anyone, because they may have to fool lovers and friends of those they replace. Easy intimacy is a quality that is rewarded. They exchange it for a tin coin, and a handful of smaller sexual wart coins that show their presence in genital disease. They infect, and are infected, as they rob their sexual partner under the night sky. They steal imprints of house keys, business cards, and look through wallets for personal addresses. They are joined together as one for a moment through sex, and are joined together as one for life, as they quickly steal what they can.

If caught, they will explain that they are providing for the baby they might have as a result of the intimacy. Their self delusional wit, they think, will charm the aggressor into submission.

If they actually had a baby, then that would be better. It would have the same blood group as the parent, should they be caught breaking in.

They will have their land back, one way or another, and fake Horis doctors will help. Herpes will become heart attacks and placebos given instead of cures.

Horis. Onus. Anus. They are pendulums that swings both ways, in both directions. The members are bi-sexual, criminal and honest, in case their doppelgangers are.

The Horis looked to her father as if he was an oracle. He was a sundial to them, with his hair and sore, and so was Ireland. The single black hair is the gnomon, which is the aurora, and his ankle sore is the sundial face, the land. His body is the time in between. He holds the secret of the forth dimension within his folds of flesh. He was a cult leader, without even knowing that he was. His double in the past was replaced by a double. A double and a double make four which is whore, as they lose their ethics and morals.

The Horis wasn't the only cult that reveres him, without knowing him. He was warlock, with his wand held by his eye brow, which is another palm. It is because there is an eye shape in his hand print. He is the magician, as the black wand disappears and appears. Abracadabra. The next generation is daubed at a distance, struck by a bolt of lightening made of cell tissue. Her father was also tarot card, and the King of all cards. In the computer age his wand becomes a stylus on his brow instead, and hair is styled, to match the name.

He hides from these mad people, who would make him a god, so that they can steal his place in the world, and become a god themselves. They are too strange and too many, with their cults and clubs that are everywhere he looks. They are easily seen through the internet and while walking through the towns. They stick to memories and buildings.

*

The chat rooms are millions in number, and no one can get bored, but everyone does. The users mingle meanings and hints to who they are. They veil themselves with forged pdfs, gpegs, and gifs, while the cut and paste program provides the chat. They do not give any part of themselves away. They are too precious, too careful, while others that do the same are

41

misleading and criminals. They are right and they are wrong. It is all that accuse the others of the same crime that they are.

*

The Horis whores thrived through fear. They loved the disasters that bring them wide eyes and open minded people, which are easier to hypnotise and are more open to suggestion. They are like, and are part of, the internet world. It is loaded with flash frames that follow shock revelations or seductive tales. They were put there by the military. They are fancy dressed as beautiful women, when they want to control the mind of men, and are handsome men when they want to control women. They slip themselves in between flashes of light and outrageous suggestion. Every computer user receives the same flashed words, no matter which chat room they have joined. It is to stimulate unity and sameness, should opposing views meet in life. They will be fooled that they are the same, by the flash words they subconsciously act out. This, it was thought, would stop murders and violence. It worked only when intimacy and friendship wasn't coveted, as if it was, the innocent would follow the violent in to bloody homes, in the illusion that they were already intimate friends and safe. The flash frames were an accidental bludgeoning of the sensibilities, instead of the promised utopia of computer control. The Horis did it on purpose.

*

Shannon's mother types wildly in thinly veiled code, so simplistic it is almost like another alphabet. She hides behind a photo of a man, to get the secrets of women she has taken a dislike to, and the secrets of teenage girls, just like the computer program does.

42

She will mould their minds while they are impressionable, and learn about their families, using their interest in men. Knowledge is power. When she is gossiping, she uses the photo of one of the women that she doesn't like. She is careful though, of what she writes, and how she writes it. She knows that she can be found, by the internet police, if she speaks freely of the crimes she has planned. The words she types are stolen phrases from the woman's life. The phrases are used as codes for meeting places and times, for friends, and for victims, polite questions. If the chat is logged, it will look like a chat bot loop.

*

As the pregnancy progresses, the laptop is balanced on the swollen hump of her mothers stomach and Shannon can feel the heat of the laptop through the womb. It burns. She can hear the fan and the key board. The keyboard sounds like squeegee damp slaps and she tries to move away from it, away from the source of heat.
Her mother eventually and quickly decides for herself that it is too uncomfortable, and Shannon is left to cool.

*

Her mother's surname was close to the sound of Horis, and begun with nearly the same arrangements of letters. Her name is what they may use to attract her, using her self love or self hate as a silent mating call. They will hold a mirror to her face by echoing her name in rhyme as she passes them. They will rhyme words, and act rhyming actions. They will show rhyming objects and events.
Horl.
Whorl meant hole, or knot, set in wood. Whorl was also a tornado under the sea, and looked like a bath emptying.

Her mother was scared of her own name, but also worshipped it. Names were power, as was appearances. If you looked like a king, in the underground world of the criminal, then you were treated as one. If your name was the same as a person who had power, then you were treated as if you had the same power.

It was the negative side that frightened her. Others would think as she did; others, who called themselves witches and twins, would use her name against her, after going through her bins, or eavesdropping at the post office. Too many people played charades as she walked past, who gave her direction with their eyes, and acted her name out. Whore, give me money, they would say in the language that had no words. The mimes, all adult, but also two or three Horis years old, needed only a nod and a look in the right direction to get their meaning across, they thought. They ate, and then spat out her name in bits, digging her conscience for rightful ownership of it. If it wasn't her name at birth, then they could steal it from her, and make it theirs, because she stole it herself. Mostly, they wanted to know whether she had fooled a family into letting her in, with a same face and same name.

*

Shannon is a four month old embryo.

Her body counted with missed periods and aurora thoughts. Her mother felt the womb grow to accommodate her. The muscles of it buckled and contorted as it widened, giving the appearance and feeling of a baby kicking at the stomach skin. It feels like one kick, two kicks, as the womb stretches. The binary language is contained in a pregnancy, the television and the internet. The one, two pattern of the machines is planned to take the full grown adult back to embryo stage, as it echoes the womb with a one / two flash of light and sound.

Her mother knows it is the womb, and not the baby that moves. One for no, two for yes. She sits at the table asking it questions. She is talking to the dead whose genes come alive again through the womb wall. The dead come to life, when there is a pregnancy, in their struggle to be born again. It is a séance as she knows it to be.

She asks whether it is safe to go to the hospital for the birth. She is worried about her life, she says. The rumours are that some doctors murder the mothers and hang the baby upside down, when it is born, as if it had just slipped out of the aurora, rather than the mother; as if the baby was diving towards the land rather than slipping out on to a sterile sheet. It is the ugliness of some of the natives that hints at this practice. Some look as if they had been squashed by something solid, and jokes become real with people that don't have humour.

It is another play on words. They have lost their humour, or their humerus. They are a bone short of humanity. They are animal like in their shortened spirit, say their accusers, as they also cannot extend a helping hand to those that need it. Their arms are too short to do this.

As if to demonstrate that the rumours are real, one of the cults has begun to hang their captive pigs the same upside down way, as if in agreement with the doctor midwives. They drain the pigs of blood by slitting their throats. It seems to be a veiled insult to the pregnant mothers and their ugly babies –the English natives are the land, and the land is shaped like a pig.

Her mother thinks the womb has answered 'yes' the next time the muscle of the womb expands, and adapts her mind to accommodate the idea.

*

When TV News flash declares another national emergency the UK is held under curfew. This means that no one is allowed outside after curfew time, which is nine o'clock, and also means that Shannon suffers another clench of muscles and a flush of unwanted adrenaline as the news is absorbed.

It is exercise for the stomach, the news is. It is watched by lazy fashion followers, who clench and unclench in the hope to achieve their desired skinniness, and by people like her mother, for that reason. They will scare their paunches in to shape, without making an effort.

There is another reason that her mother sits through the frightening scenes. She wants to scare the life-giving blood out of her baby, and into herself. She will push the blood with a quickened heart beat, so it rushes through the baby, with no time to feed it nutrients, and rest only when it is returned. It is rightfully hers. The blood was life giving. It would renew cells that had long died, if it skipped the baby. Clench and thou should have eternal life. Fright made the stomach curl and tighten. If she aborted the baby late it was even better for her skin and the oestrogen would make her breasts larger. She will drink the milk they produced herself. It was nectar from the gourds. Her nipples were twin fountains of youth sitting on top of their hills. The milk was cloudy magical water.

The curfew is announced because of night time scavengers breaking and ransacking abandoned and flooded premises. Everyone is tired of everything. Everything has stopped working, except the air planes that arrive every week that the winds don't, with travellers that don't go home.

Some people wonder in a half hysteric joking way, whether the power cuts are planned. The decisions, apparently made at the top of the organisations that are in control, have been so ill thought out, that sanity is questioned. They wonder if they are being captured on digitised film for army scientists who missed the panic on their faces before. A recording for robots to ape, and computer programs to organise, perhaps. Panic, tears, and smile, like an old film of the Oscars awards, shot out at double quick time. It is also because, just before the television switches itself off this time, there is a painting. The painting, a woman in a crown, seems to be another arty interpretation of the UK. The woman has red hair sitting above a pale rouged face and has a potato blight pattern sprawled underneath her in the form of a dress. The painting was banned along time in the past, says the presenter, for echoing the Horis. The piled up hair is the aurora sky, when the painting is turned upside down. The blight eyes are sitting in the sky, on their background of velvet blue, on top of the aurora. It was painted yesterday, and hundreds of years ago, and now it will be banned again, if they realise, because now it seems to show the position of spy satellite cameras in its eye pattern, and secret mobile masts in the background, disguised as ships.

The painting is a play on words too. On a dress is spying. They are spying on addresses. They like to play on words, the media does, to let the public know they understand their own play on words; their rhyming slang, their cryptograms, and anagrams. Their literal interpretation of the English language is shown in a hopscotch cartoon, full of chalk letters. It is a play on words.

The public also wonder whether it was the last glance at the past, before their world is given light again. The electricity is turned off, and there is no heating, no electricity or clean water, and what a contrast when the lights are turned on. It could be a viewing event for the privileged, a millennium count down to civilisation, seen by a private satellite, while the public CCTV is locked out.

It is announced in the newspapers the next day that there is a group of criminals from overseas that have been allowed to wonder freely around England. They do not want descriptions of themselves circulated when they have committed a crime, especially the colour of their hair. It is discrimination, they say, to state blonde, brown, grey or black. The article is written in a serious way and is front page news.

The reports continue with: they are roaming the country with the intent of cattle farming, and the populace are the cattle. They treat others like disobedient pets, and can not understand why they do not behave like monkeys. When they take homes illegally, they are genuinely disturbed and outraged when they are evicted and arrested, and say it was empty, apart from the animals. The newspapers advise care in opening the knocked door. The authorities have been informed but are under staffed. The curfew becomes old news as the new News is swallowed. The television works again for a few hours to repeat the same news story.

The chemicals in the body bubble.

The country is being aborted. There is a whole generation of embryos lost to the rhythm of the BBC news chimes.

Chapter 3

It can be a bewildering walk from the home to the shops, no matter how familiar the route is, when the route has been strewn with people. They blink too meaningfully in too many directions to make sense to anyone who isn't interested in them. The uncomfortable feeling of forced intimacy lingers, and there is an incomprehensible meaning for their darting looks. They all don't talk at once, and the sound is deafening.

Most people know the silent language. It is used by good and bad alike, and before a baby can use their voice. It is a useful way to communicate in storms and factories, where the voice disappears in to the void, and, in the illness of the body, no painful effort is needed to chat.

Most people use the head to talk. In other words, their eyes do not linger past the neck. They are careful, wary and polite. Each word they communicate is calculated for safety. They will talk and gesture too, if needed. There are no concrete rules, and no strictness in their method of communication. To look past the neck, and to use the body is to show an intimacy though, that could be mistaken for closeness and a relationship. The body language is the language of whores and thieves. It is also the language the butcher uses. Some use it innocently in a glance, or flirtation, but the ones that are intent on de humanising will use it constantly and coldly. The difference is the gentle nudge of a good friend, to the pawing and clawing of a stranger intent on procuring money. That is how it feels when the looks are unwanted. As if they have tried to grab at a passing limb.

It is no coincidence; they want to be the one who isn't said no to, the one that's is lawfully intimate.

If they know their target has children, then they will become as the child. If they are closer to the mother, then they will be as the mother. They do it gradually, over the years, until one day the target will smile an acceptance into their world.

Voodoo, and viewed you again.

They have watched them as they have watched the television. The look of intimacy that slips out of the eyes that is finally acknowledging will bring the prize for the criminals. The prize is the purse, the car, the home; their life and children.

The criminals are everyday obstacles, but when the world is in shock, then everyone has the language of the eyes, everywhere. It blurbs out of people with the innocence of babies, wide eyed and unsure of everything. The criminals scream their intent without using their tongue, immigrants reveal where they are from with sidelong looks and exaggerated expressions, housewives speak silently their day time TV language, and everyday people will accidentally tell of irrelevant incidences that make up their hours, as a stray glance meets other eyes for a few seconds.

All are friends and all are enemies.

And the CCTV tapes the chaos.

The army analyse and pin point who is who. They shift and collaborate. The public are GPS ed, and DNA ed, without feeling a thing.

The damage is already done, when everyone is in shock. The next seed of thought is planted. The hidden show their face, and step in paths. It only takes a second to tell what they want, and they are gone.

Shock, shock, everyday in every way. With a brain state near to concussion, and eyes open wide, they replace original knowledge with their own message, re teaching everyone to be an echo of themselves.

Shannon will have to be careful, with their trusting eyes, that turn and twist with secrecy. She will echo because she doesn't understand why they have stopped her or made eye contact. She won't understand why the whore will show a mutilated breast to the priest or why the child will scream for help, when she is not in danger. She won't understand why dead bodies have been broadcasted across the country so doesn't understand mind control. She will walk away and her eyes will dart and echo with the would-be assailants message, and the message that was conveyed to her would be spread. She would have become an unwitting virus.

*.

The statues in the church have been designed carefully, before they have been chosen for the plinths. They are to focus on, to steady the eyes, before meeting another person. For those that want to know what they have been told, the statue is substitute limbs and undefended eyes, as the looks of strangers are repeated upon it rather then friends and family.

Then they are on their knees again, to see what the child sees after being in the rush of people. Children are the most easily influenced, because of their eagerness for life, and are targeted more. They are trapped by easy smiles, and parental familiarity, to be confused later by doubles, who will claim to have known them well in their childhood.

When they rest their eyes from the busyness of wild stares, they rest them from bright clothes, and from waving arms too. They are advised to focus on the stillness of a statue, so they may show the same stillness to others. The statues are saints or similars.

Another statue is Mary and the baby. Mary is the Virgin, and the whore as people try to interpretate what the baby seller or the friendly mother has communicated to them. It is hard to see sometimes which ones are which, they think, and greet both with the same blank politeness, until they know what they are being told.

Pregnant women look with love and attention towards the statue of Mary and the baby, in the hope that their baby will be born in the image of the baby statue. They believe the baby takes its image from their eyes so stare at the well formed. They want their babies to grow with full arms and legs, with an undamaged face. They spend hours in front of the statue, and some have mini statuettes propped on top of their televisions, so that the icon is within their eyesight the whole time. They are forgivably extreme in their devotion towards their embryo. When they don't have icons, they have photos of loved ones propped on top of the TV. Their eyes will gravitate towards that in between the flashing lights of the telly, and influence the baby instead of the box. No one wants a flickering picture as a child, and they are scared that it is what it will become without direction.

The church goers also sing hymns to gently exercise the womb, in preparation for the birth, and to lull the embryo to sleep. Head up, and back straight. Take a deep breathe. Be ready for the scare that will try to make your child let go of life, and hope that the womb is strong enough to hold it. Be strong and be brave, in your pelvic muscles, so it does not shudder at the world on your behalf, and let go of the baby before it is ready to be born.

The statue of Jaesus is unfashionably in the centre of the church. It used to be the statue relegated to the sanctuary, as a reminder of the need for cleanliness and isolation in illness. It is the oldest type of statue any church has and is the figure that depicted the stigmata and old age, with their shared symptoms; the indentation of the crown of thorns, the marks of tied wrists, the sign of a nail in the ankle, the bleeding rib…

The list of ailments that Shannon has to remember so that she recognises her own body is too long, and she forgets.

The Jaesus statue was for studying the blight and old age. The Chrystians thought the two were connected. The original statues displayed the darkened age spots that formed on old heads and bodies. They looked like stretched leopard skin. They were liver marks around the crown of the head. They looked like drops of dried, stained blood, as if the crown of thorns had been removed. The brown drops dripped on to wrinkled wrists and made them look as if rusty hand cuffs had been taken off. Tiny veins crossed on the hands and feet, where circulation was stifled, to take the appearance of the crucifixion. Skin split, through wear and tiredness. It was longevity or leper. The blight was both, they thought, but in infancy. If they rid the body of it, then old age could be delayed.

There was another reason for the aged appearance of the old Jaesus statue. Some people never thought that the human lived that long. They had never seen wrinkles or stringy veins. They thought dying young and human sacrifice was normal. It had been all a jumble of superstition and stupidity before they had been shown age by example. Previous rumours of Chrystianity had involved death wreathes and embalming, not picturesque sculpturing. The death wreath, that had been shaped to echo the ring of liver spots around the head, had been a wish for others to die of the same old age, but had turned into savage beads in the retelling. The beads were given to wear around the head instead. Wearing them would make the wearer grow to an old age, said the sellers, and believed it too; that they had the power of giving age by the use of them. They looked, at a distance, as if they could be age spots, they thought.

The statue became younger, later, when the study of transfiguration was added to its list of uses. The spontaneous bleeding started as the outstretched arms reached the edge of the universe. It recorded planets and stars as bumps in the skin, on its journey through space, and the world was measured out in inch worm and equatorial spacing along the forehead. It showed the transfiguration, caught in motion– of the world from the universe, and of the human from the animal. The blood rib, that will appear and disappear overnight, is another space border crossed.

It sits just under the top layer of skin, exaggerated on the statue, so that it can be seen better, just under the ribs. It is as thin as a paper cut, but not as deep. A mere miracle of a graze. It stretches out, seemingly appearing when no one is looking, and heals itself just as shyly. It will happen once a year, on Shannon, every year, at the same time, conjuring a connection with the aurora, just like her fathers blemishes does.

Shannon has all of the stigmata, though.

She is the Chrystian Calendar.

She is the lost book of Jaesus, and of the Holy Ghost.

Some of the symptoms will come and go in her yearly remaking, but some will be solid and be with her until death. Her crown of ghostly thorns can be slightly seen - her pinpoint, her line of latitude, is her thorn embedded.

Her penny sores are other thorns that have scratched her from underneath.

The tiny sacred heart, bulgy and pink, is sitting on her tiny chest, and will also be with her until death. It is the sacred heart of Mary. She thinks she is a joke. The Mary don: meridian, of the sacred Hertz.

The sacred heart has a religious cross that is in the centre of it.

The claddagh ring, with it's outstretched hands, which are the ribs, seemingly holding the heart in place, explains itself with one look at her own chest. It is a micro mosaic relic to the power of Jaesus. Shannon also thinks though, that it is a vain attempt at survival disguise. Her heart is exposed already, so it doesn't need cutting open. It sits on top of the bony plinth of the sternum, as a sacrifice to medicine.

She has other marks that will always be with her. The brown mole sits on the front of her ankle, on just one leg. It is a sign of the crucifixion, the crucible of the joining. It is a permanent mar.

She is Cinderella. Her foot wears one Georgian slipper, and it can only be seen by the same dainty, small brown button. It is made of glass. Her father's ankle wears its side buckle, and is wearing the other slipper. It takes her father's family centuries to get dressed in the clothes of the air. Her blue veins will dance as she runs, separating green foliage back into blues and yellows, the same as she is. She is a novice photo-shop J peg. She will walk among the CCTV's and not be there at all, because all she is are stories. Food that she needs will float away into nothingness. She has been sworn as guilty, before she is born, because of her skin. She will be arrested for intention. Her stocking mask is already half pulled up from her face, and sits on her forehead permanently, and her head has been handcuffed for thinking of a crime.

A pattern of moles sits in the shape of Orion on her lower arm, and an upside down question mark, just above it. Her mole bi-plane, which sits under her breasts, is another cross.

Her body tells her about her body, by actions, rather than words. It will start again at the beginning when it has finished.

The graze on the rib will come and go, as will the paper cut grazes on her fingers. There is more that will appear and disappear, everyday. There is three hundred and sixty five marks, varying in size and shape that will make up her year, then her body will be back to the beginning again.

Shannon is a baking potato struck with blight. Old age is fungi and a mushroom ring. All the other vegetables will have the blight too. She will be called a vegetable when she is born. Two vegetables, as her face is two different sizes. She will be meat and two veg. A spaceman's foiled wrapped all-in-one. A take-away in a tray, when she slips out. A shiny tin tray, so she will be able to have one glance at the object that she has heard about, herself, before her oxygen disappears.

*

Jeasus didn't die on the cross, he died because of the cross infected. It is food contaminated, it is person infected. It is scabies on the hairline, and impetigo too.

*

The inflicted used the Jaesus statue to compare boils, as they pointed out their maladies on varying stone limbs, and said where theirs had grown or shrunk in the same places. It only took the right conditions for them to become the same ill.

In the United Kingdom and Ireland, the Jaesus statue was sitting in the centre, where the Horis would have had it. The weather was hurricane, blizzard, hot and wet; A predictable pattern of unpredictability. They were waiting for blight to strike the crops, the animals and the congregation. The jaesus statue was a warning of it.

The statue was used for a calendar too. The bleeding rib of Jaesus, occurred on the human, herself, at the beginning of the early harvest, in the short summer. The statue was used to arrange meeting times and places, just as repetitive internet pages were.

In some churches the centre of the raised dais, where the statue now stands, was also seen as the land point of the aurora. It is imagined to be in front of the stained glass windows, which are normally shaped with three arches. These are seen as three fingers or the three Muses. The three muses are also continents. Some churches have a priest door, next to the stage. The Horis called this the thumb door, because of its special relationship with the windows. There are old caricature drawings of fat monks with their stomachs stuck out, in an impersonation of the imagined priest emerging. The bright red robes of the priests, with its white short cloak, are laughed at by the Horis. He, the priest, is a thumb and white nail, emerging from a thumb hole. The monks, similarly dressed, but in shades of grey, are dirty thumbs. The drawings are a trophy of their invasion of the church. The monks have a ring of hair, rather than a ring of liver spots or thorns. They are not old or ill, but are a slowly changed tableau.

The thumb is the only part of the hand that mostly resembles the whole of the body, they think. It, like most spines, bends only forward, and the fingers are its ribs. They are born with their hearts in their hands, they say. The outline of it is in the lines of the palm, waiting to be enclosed by finger digit ribs and attached to lungy mounds of the thumb, should the miracle of life happen in a thunder and lightning prophesy.

Any part of the body can become another human though, they think. They populate the world by standing still, they say, and the aurora light, that makes them alive, colours and shapes the world and its people by looking at their image. Breasts become Buddhas, and shins become Mongolians. Aboriginals are other heads, and arms become long legged blondes. They are hand, fingers and thumbs all over the world as well as being the god and goddesses of it.

The Chrystian Jaesus is the Horis's placebo god, which stands patiently in their place, to keep the world and people in the right shape.

They imagine, the aurora worshippers, that the triangle of the palm print would be the centre of the church stage, and also the imagined balancing point and sixty degree corner of the aurora. They are intermingled in their mind. The aisle is the crease that runs from the triangle of the palm towards the wrist. The folds of the inside wrist are the pews. The thumb can never touch the centre of the palm, just as humans can never touch the aurora. The priest apes the thumb, as he stands to one side, raised on the pulpit. His raised figure will cast a shadow that will span the triangle that is in front of the three fingered windows. It will seem that his thumb shadow is laying down, horizontally, on the aurora. The aurora is the womb, and the thumb, the smallest of them all, is the baby in the womb. They will still be the baby when they grow old, counting with aurora years. They will reach the aurora through their shadow, after death. It is their holy grail, their heaven that is Valhalla.

But it is their fury that takes them in to aurora while they are living. The blood boils and sweats as they rage against the world. It rises up, as heat, to make the skies red. To anger others, to feed the aurora, is some of their purpose on earth.

The Horis understands all this, but the priests do not. The Horis are obsessed by their vision of what was the architectural inspiration for the churches. Chrystians, they say, do not understand the ceremonies and customs that they play out. They are the invaders of the church, who copied and pinched the buildings and rituals. The aurora is the hand, and the hand is the womb, and the womb is the aurora, nothing else.

*

They think they are all and everything, but the Chrystians are politicians. They assimilate. The church absorbs the enemy, and changes it. The enemy will not hurt what it thinks is itself. They will listen to the priest, when they think it is one of them that are speaking, and the priest teaches them another truth, using their icons as his own.

*

The dust from farming covers the skin in a fine layer that is almost invisible. It enters every orifice, including the eyes, without being noticed. The fine muslin, wrapped around the face, protects but isn't enough. It is a second skin of earthy richness. The dust protects the skin from the sun, like dried up tropical suntan oil and looks natural, until the sweating starts. The forehead is crying clay blood. They shower most of it off, but it stays in the eyes, making them gritty and bitty. It gathers in the corners and occasionally drops out in stone tears.

Their skin starts to gain a hue of soil, the colour dependent on the area they live in or the crop they are pulling up. They are a light rainbow of people of yellow, green, orange, red and brown, squinted eyed and slightly exotic. Their hair is coloured by the sun and the over chlorinated pool water, leaving it in shades of gold and cream, adding to their water colour pallet. They nit comb it every night, and mostly keep it short.

When the petrol shortage is over, they will gain normality, and lose their varying tints. They will feel lucky that they were only needed for a year or two, and that their lives were not dominated by the turn of the seasons. They have seen the photos of children born to the older farm workers, and their deformities. They have seen x rays of their lungs, riddled with

60

insecticide and dead dust, and photos of infected cuts. They know they are lucky not to have the same fate or life.

The shower cubicles, pulled on to the farms as emergency equipment, block quickly, and there is a puddle of water that the temporary farmers paddle in as they wash, collecting warts and slivers of sharp corn.

To clear the blockage, the farmer's children will shove sticks down them after school, and develop conjunctivitis.

There is an antibiotic shortage, as the newspapers claim racial sabotage from minorities. Another domineering headline is crisp flavours, as the trains in the UK stop running.

Look down instead of up. Look left instead of right. Don't look around at your new neighbours. Don't notice.

*

The emergency farmers, who are local Chrystians, sleep.
They are too good for the bad.
They are called grasshoppers, locusts and cockroaches, depending on the dirt colour of their skin. Their parents were called frogs and toads. They all jump and crouch, and are all ready to climb ropes. They are sea worthy and athletic trained, with wrinkled, skeletal faces and shocked round eyes, just like the generation before.

Their comparisons, the insects, creep into the houses with the winds, and make weird noises during the night. The noises sounds like the word 'shit', repeated over and over again, with the tongue sticking to the roof of the mouth and said between gritted teeth. Shit..... Shit.... Shit, and when the sleepers awake, there it is coming out of the toilet as the drains block.

The blocked drains are happening all over the country, and there are UK evacuees teaching their children how to live outside. It is a fatalistic acceptance of the situation. A new moving generation is born. They circle the UK in an endless progression, echoing Russian caravans while they adapt to a possible new way of living.

They collect rain water to shower in, remember trails, make notes of flooded fords and eat vegetables grown en route. They make friends with people who own nuclear bunkers, and overseas visitors that live in Dutch barges. They are ready for a new beginning, but prefer clean washing machines, steady jobs and the normal life. They hold festivals in eternal hope that music will heal the air with extra heat.

They pass by, on the TV, close to where Shannon is.

There are photos of Afghan coats, dripping, smiling faces, and discussions on whether a festival will continue, as there is a curfew. The women wear their hair and dresses long, and look like story book princesses as they travel to the site of the festival.

The festival is at the fairy tale building of Knebworth House, and they look like a collection of auditions, as they stare at the sky.

They know they are looking at the weather, but to others they seem to be looking at the powder pink turrets in romantic longing. The men are weary, leather clad bikers. They fight the stormy rain and slippery roads. In between gatherings they organise hidden, all night barbeques, and supply solar powered radios to the travellers. Some of the other festival goers are fakes, there to watch the families they had spied on in previous years. They want to see if any of their habits have changed.

They dress and behave the way their mothers and fathers did. They have late eighteen hundred style side burns, and the women are still half hiding their invisible expensive opera glasses in the folds of hand sewn dresses. They are as starey as the other cults, and they too tape with their eyes.

They are all mindless copy cats, too frightened to be themselves. They copy the people who seem able to survive, and the people who are more popular. Their clothes are feathers and fur, and they evolve as people are watching. In their minds eye, they are already looking at their ancestors as they look around, spotting their next set of skins and kins.

The cults are popular in their uniformity of thinking and dress. People can get lost in them, and merge as different people. They can hide their true feelings and thoughts within a cloak of conformity, so they can shake off anyone willing to replace them. Everyone wants to hide from the spying doppelganger who will swap with them, if they could. The worse the behaviour the cult has, then the less likely it is that there will be a double following. It is hide and seek, and ID I seek.

The land invites shadows following shadows, with it's isolation from the mainland, its shape, its foggy air, and mysterious skies. The dress of the festival goers apes the thought. It isn't their fault again; the blame of crime lies within the land and its mysticism.

Shannon feels movement, and faints.

The copy cats are part Horis, part 'viewed you'. They copy, and wait for the catastrophe, before stepping into someone else's life.

They are the same cult as any other. Only snobbery and habitat separates the groups. They have convinced themselves they are herd and grab at self pity at the inevitable truth. One individual is replaceable as the next, in their cult. They think it is reasonable to watch another build their life and possessions, and to take their place in the world, before their place, in turn, is taken. It is the law of the jungle, and they will make the jungle where ever they want it to be. They warp words and laws to fit in with their life style, and are mostly disliked by all. They dress exactly to whom they have targeted, and match hair cuts and personality with expert skill. They hope to be mistaken for the stalked, to test their acting and mimicry skills. The slaughter house is bigger and warmer, they moo at each other with words and without, and nod in another's direction. It reads, and looks like, 'daughter's house.' or 'laughter house'. When they hear or see it mimed, they think it is an instruction, and fool like clowns, laughing their way past slippery corners, not knowing what danger they are in, thinking it is always others that are.

Welcome to my daughter's house, the enemy says, without making a sound.

Herd has no laws, and therefore cannot be convicted of crimes. They are free of crime and conscience, and they have given up humanity in favour of being a shadow, an echo, of it. They do not like people like Shannon because she will be born with an individuality that cannot be copied. Her disappearance would be noticed, and someone will then have to do something. What cult can not be, cult ridicules. She will be called goat, sheep and bull, because of her brows. Her ancestors must have been looked at so closely, for them to know. Their genetics were closer to meat than to a person, the cult had said, and had accused the mothers of bestiality. They will name her animal too, and say she should not own a home or possessions, as they have said before, and try to take both away.

A cult scorned,

is a cult warmed.

Their anger knows no end. It echoes from generation to generation, then the cult takes it's civilisation off, like it is a fancy dress, when their tricks don't work. When the rabid pack have torn apart an animal they hide the crime by pulling the animals skin over themselves, and wait ready to attract the next meal, say the nature programmes, and the cult copy what they see. They have fancy dress after fancy dress to slip into, and each fancy dress is a parody of their last victim.

They will steal her mask with Boots counter make up, and eyebrow pencil. They will have her wonky head with asymmetrical haircuts, and have her crooked smile with their own muscles. They will hide in loose crowds to tempt in the next nearly extinct.

*

Shannon awakes in another part of the county. She has edged a millimetre or so, in the measurements of maps, and a mile or so in the measurement of foot. She is the size and shape of a frog. From a flea to a locust, to a frog.

Her mother and father have escaped the merging festival hordes and have decided to visit the space ship instead, which hovers discreetly above a close village. It is thought the space ship is a hole in the ozone which reflects the shape of the earth, or a weather satellite that is fighting for control of the weather. There had been experiments on how to control the weather for years. The weather is the very cold meeting the very hot. It is the household machines and the central heating that makes the heat, the public are told, which meets the cold air off the sea, which makes the hurricanes. To control the weather, it is a matter of physics. Electricity is off here, the electricity is on there. If there is no heat at all, then England would slip into Icelandic temperatures, if there is too much heat, England slips into gales and blizzards. The military is Thor, it is thought, playing with the energy and power of the skies, thumping a finger down on a keyboard as if it were a wooden club. The public is made to think though, that the world is controlled by the cooking of Sunday dinner and the boiling of a kettle. The 'space ship' or weather satellite has a jokey appearance of a cloud ball hidden by a cartoon cloud, which gives the impression it is army controlled camouflage. It is the same icon that appears on TV weather reports predicting cloud and sunshine. It lies under the exosphere, on level with other clouds.

Shannon can hear what is seen louder here, and thinks the space ship that is talking to her.

The sky, the voice says, is full of clouds shaped as old TV shows and cartoons. They float like an air carousel, appearing as regular as the aurora. There are cats, and eyes, and weather clouds, ghost and dinosaurs, each with their regular time and theme. They too are the calendar of someone, of everyone. You are not alone, Shannon. It knows how her skin speaks, she thinks, as it does the same. Her skin is the sky, because the sky became her skin, with breathed in chemicals and broadcasted delusions.

Here, says the voice, is her fathers favourite place. It is on the brow of a hill that has opposing paths. On one path there is a family of handicapped rabbits. No one knows why they are handicapped, they just are, and always have been. On the other side is a field of windy yellow flowers, whose pollen fills the air with perfume. In spring the field looks like a green, wavy sea, made of land. In summer, it will look like the fur of a fox, with hints of red over brown. After it has been reaped, it becomes the illegals fabled bed of nails. Shorn straw, as evenly spaced as velcro, is their outside bed which they sleep on. There is an illegal in every field, it is thought, and they whistle warnings at each other when it is dark. Each plans to have a field to own when the opportunity arises. They wait like the Horis do, for the worst of the weather, to make their move.

This time they block the emergency showers and toilets. The action is shown by the appearance of the unravelled, unused toilet rolls, which have been hooked on to the brambles that run the length of the hedge of the field. Someone put it there to say something. It is a message. Some people talk, some people talk without speaking, and some use props to talk. Her father and mother have paused to look at the white streak, and it is obvious, to Shannon at least, what the message is. 'The white reek'.

There is a feeling of floating as they move away from the distraction from the usual. Shannon becomes the air. She is mobile communication and she is in the womb. It is a second of longing to see the colour yellow, and to see the colour green, and the white markings of toilet roll, that spurs her, but most of all she wants to be as fast as the machine in the air, that, she thinks has just swept over and brushed everyone with air waves. It is wind without speed or sound, gluey in minute membranes.

She is dreaming but is there. She doesn't move but knows exactly where she is with a clarity that is almost like sight, and her features change slightly, so that she resembles a cat, which is the next living thing whose size she will match. It is another useless, un-chameleon like change, and she unknowingly smiles at her arsenal of slight morphic disguises. You, she says to the spaceship, with her skin, are this; and shows it the red grazes on her fingers. You gave life like this, she adds, and points with her finger, because when you made this, this happened. Her body shows it, by actions of little cuts appearing here and there, disappearing and re appearing, in a sequence that it understands, but she doesn't.

But it is all over in a second, and she falls into a deeper sleep.

Chapter 4

The letters, if they can be called letters, appear raised on the skin, like gentle braille, written by the hand of Jaesus. They are not the English alphabet letters yet, but are a hint of them.

The priests and nuns, of the dimly lit past, studied the spots and moles on anyone willing to be studied. They orbited the body, taking notes, and the Greek alphabet is invented. It is called the Greek language after the island that sits at the toe of Italy, because that is the amount of warty water man needs to drink to change his bio chemistry. The name is a comparison The letters are rudimentary, and time and copying haven't yet formed their shape into everyday use.

Shannon has the alphabet and grammar in her timed paper cuts and bruises. The punctuation they are appears between the mole letters. It consists of disappearing bloody commas, full stops, colons and semi colons. They denote and dictate small pieces of time. With the natural raised brow of age, they also make up the expletives and diacritics of the grammatical world; the asterisk and bullet, the caret, daggers, dashes and brackets. The moles are illustrated in brown ink; their colour, shape and size are full stops. The grammar is in red ink because that is the colour of the bleeding grazes and spots that appear and disappear on her. Their appearance causes short bursts of surprise at tediously repetitive intervals. They make the writer pause as they invade the hand, and it is studied for its splitting. They are thought to stop the skin from gibbering its message, just as grammar does in the English language. Some letters are also drawn in red ink, depending on the shape of the cut that appears.

The dashes and full stops appear on her arm when it is over exerted, she thinks, and sweaty. It is the yearly S.O.S of the Morse code. Dash, dot, dash, dot. She needs help, in the squashy womb she is in. Women and children first. Dash dot dash.

She will be born and run through fields of pollen with a second skin of clothes, which will protect her from bites and brambles. The sweat will change her distress call, and imprint it on the material. The dots and dashes will rush to the nearest corner of her arm, in the crook of her elbow, leaving a sweaty print as an open number four. It will look like a squashed leggy, flying aphid. It is camouflage and a warning for the countryside. She will hide among the number insects and Roman numeral leafs, flexing her stained elbow to scare bees away.

*

The nuns and monks asked questions of parentage and siblings as they prodded and measured the blemishes. They made notes of cousins and couplings. They traced the family tree and put together the whole of the sentence they hope has formed between kin, on the skin. It is a sign, and a symbol of the heavens perhaps. A message from the skies. God exists, hears and replies.

Praise be to God. God can hear and answers through the chosen.

Raise your voice to the heavens, and they will reply to you through another's skin. For those who chose not to speak, this was proof that they weren't meant to. The message of Jaesus, on the skin, is a message to the world, from God, their father.

May God be with you. They would have watched from generation to generation.

She would have belonged to god, and would have carried the message of the Lourdes upon her skin. She would have been forbidden to do anything, in case a letter was changed. She would have been queen and had willing servants; she would have been an amusement and an ever lasting discovery as she crowned herself anew every year, with her ticker tape skin.

She would have had one lover, her husband, and a multitude of children. They would have studied each other, like animals do, and would have waited for the message to be completed in their grandchildren. She would have been anointed with oils, but her skin would have stayed parched with a thirst that could not be quenched. Her skin, and her children's skin, would have been the new parchments, and the scribe of the parchments would have belonged to the church. They would have adopted her because of pity and a thirst for knowledge, and her skin changing would have paid for her nourishment.

*

Shannon knows it all, and nothing, while her mother and father are standing in the village field.

She knows of a satellite program that has gone wrong, of screaming in the night, and that her mother is a paedophile who abuses and sells children. She passes out, and hopes she has misunderstood.

*

They will shove themselves in her, because she has been in one of them. Then after they have been in her, she will be back in them, as food. She is in, out, in, out, bake it all about. They think no one will notice how they exchange places with her,

71

using the words of a simpleton. She will be born again, through the backside, they will say, and will wait for another child to appear who answers to the same name, as she disappears as shit. Her birth certificate will be given to a baby the same colour, they say, so there is no difference. They mean an immigrant.

*

Her mother is a Horis, and her father a Chrystian.

Her mother is full of hatred for his genetic programming, which she lacks. She would have to pay to be infected, through semen, dirty water and shit, so she can produce the letters and pictorials on her skin that were envied hundreds of years before.

Her mother has small black eyes and, when she has had a course of antibiotics, her skin becomes thick pink and white. Her hair is lustrous but she brushes it harshly to produce the illusion of split hairs and a darker ancestry. She wants people to know she is back; back from the dead, back from being an older version of herself. Back rhymes with black, and she is telling the truth with her hair. Honesty breeds honesty, and she will be told it because of the little bit of hers that she has displayed, she hopes.

She believes in the power of the television, and that her enviable husband talks like a cow, without words. She has sex with other men, and the children she has produced with them are plain. Her husband's children morph with the broadcasts, she thinks. It is their slightly Persian and Mongolian features and their quick ability to resemble the actors that pass in front of their eyes that make her think of them with disgust and jealousy. Each morph child is punctuated with a plain child.

They are dot and dash, dot and dash, like Shannon's arm. The television is his partner in their making.

Her mother's thoughts jumped to extremes. Adrenaline and hormones rush, and rush. She was taught, her mother, that extremities of moods would burn calories away too. Flight or fight to combat the fat, as she sat on her arse and waited for it to disappear. Frowns and smiles to exercise the facial muscles, so wrinkles would fade, were recommended, so she raged at the world, then laughed in a cackle, in quick succession, as if it would make up for a forgotten daily routine.

Her father accepted her moods as a natural progression from listening to the worlds same opinion. He was hero worshipped and scorned, sometimes in the same breathe; from being raised up as God's to being the spawn of the Devils, from being one of the chosen few, to being the most unhygienic. They had drunk the nectar of the gods, which were the unwashed berries of the woodland, to achieve their spots; they had eaten tiny bees and their eggs; bees sperm makes the perm; they were hives for the flies; they were liars, without saying a word. Their doctors had said there was no god, with no message and no transfiguration, but still, the same scratchy eyes wanted to believe there was. The lord giveth faith, and the lord taketh it away, in a practised routine. His body had been their temple, and, as the wind howled and the fireplaces burnt the last of the coal, some still looked at him with hope in their eyes, as the schizophrenic public opinion hailed his type again, as saviours. He was a wise man of the wild; he knew the safest routes, and what food to eat; he was the dam builder, the fire-fighter, and the food provider; he would save them in the hurricanes; he had drunk contaminated water and lived; he was naturally inoculated against the world's ills, through generations of the same habits.

He was no longer seen as the thief in the orchard, but regarded as the natural owner of it, as illegal immigration stories shot hope through the newspapers. He knew the land as an immigrant couldn't. Hysteria made him hero, and he hid in the arms of her mother, in denial, as she clung to him in rage.

He was a Chrystian through his features. Chrystians couldn't lie. It was their appearance. Each one was individual with their blemishes, even ones they shared. Each generation was born slightly differently from the last.

Thou shall not lie, said the voice, because you can't. Your father is full of morals and mars, because there is no advantage in him to be any different. He stands alone in a room full of doppelgangers and thinks they have the same mind as him. He is wrong, but is happier than they will be, and that is what saves him.

They are mostly instinct and incest; white mice and brown rats, replacing themselves in a maze, chasing the tail that looks like their own, and thinking that it has always been theirs. They live with sadness, looking at the mirror maze that isn't there.

You, Shannon will be the same. The mice and rats do not move, but do, and replace themselves with the same tales. You will stand apart, and know by looking in, where your father once stood. There will be a space that others glimpse at, or give reverence to, as they impersonate the rodent before, the one they thought they was.

It is calculus and trigonometry as you guess what he held in his hand, or who he looked at. He will be your Mars, when he is gone, and your astrology, as you calculate his time, distance and position in their world of still movement.

He will be a transfiguration that studied a transfiguration, which can never capture itself, because it is a transfiguration.

Remember Shannon, continued the voice, that they do not think the same. They may mistake you for one of themselves and take your place or turn on you as a warm swarm.

And as you are watching for his past, you will be watched by them yourself, while they are being watched by themselves.

Her mother, the little white mouse, swarmed by herself, and waited for the rest to join her. Kiss and hiss, cry and lie. She blamed the cinema and radio for her choice in husband, and said it took over her simple mind, confusing it with issues of trust and truth. Her guide had been the Horis, and to hear louder voices had been upsetting.

She had taken the double path as not to upset either of her mentors, and alternated sexual infecting strangers with loyal, monogamous relations with her husband, picking pockets with donating to charity, and tried to buy red lipstick occasionally, to help Avon war widows.

Before they could breathe and talk, a catalogue of worldly disasters filled up the time, and suddenly they were in their forties, standing in a field, still strangers to each other.

And Shannon was faint and knowing.

They probably had met in a church, as the Horis often disguised themselves as Chrystians, as well as others, and interlaced their lives with them. They loved betrayal. It is the shape of the letters, and the way the word seems to command. ' Be tale' it says. It is a definite word, in their world of uncertainty. It is the length of the land, with 13 hidden in the

'B', and it is a demand for a dramatic story. The 'B' is the hooked spear in the back of the pig english, as they twist it in. 'Be tail' it says and makes them the animal they betray.

*

There is two ghostly shadows of Ludo game pieces, floating over a road that is quite near. They are invisible to the eye, like she is. They are real and unreal triangles, topped with a ball, which floats around in hyper space.

Her mind, for a moment, mistakes them for her parents, and she can not help changing a little, to be like them too.

The nearby water towers look like tiddly winks from the air and a few fields away the same Ludo piece shape had been burnt in to the grass, with, people presumed, chemicals. It was on the ground beneath a sheltering, tree, a bright lime yellow, looking like an outline of a cartoon corpse. It was the new icon of the last generation. It lay in the corner of a field and was worshipped by Google website devotees and lost tourists.

It is a physical cryptic message, they think. 'Two ludo' is 'ludo two'. It is rhyming slang for 'you know too'. The ludo piece lying down is; you know lying. It is also voodoo, when they pronounce the 'dough' as 'do'. It is a joke, and a work of art; a local playing with the squares of fields, after the google camera left it's ghostly double shadow in hyperspace.

For a second or two Shannon thinks she is there, a ludo piece, looking up at the equally limey leafed tree, at the blued sky above. Then she is floating, travelling the roads and lanes. The Ludo pieces, she thinks, are weather symbols; hot and cold fronts meeting each other. She has left her kebab outline, as that is what the ludo piece also looks like, behind her in the field, and her dad has left a dark shadow of himself under a tree. His usable skin is a tossed sundial, and he is in its shadow.

It is a nightmare.

*

Her father is are worn by another cult, who are the block-coloured people. They take his personality as their shade of history, and the cowl, once worn by priests, as proof of it. They wear it because they do not like the tones and shades that the sun would bring to their skin and hair, they say. They do not admire the golds, reds and yellow hairstyles of the exposed, nor their tinted sun-kissed appearance. It is because they cannot obtain it and don't want to help in the fields. They wear the cowl, which is black and long, obsessively. It covers everything, apart from their feet and eyes.

That, Shannon, hints at their darkest thoughts. All they see is feet meat, when they look round. They are a rhyming slang and literal in misunderstanding meaning.

Their skin, neither sensitive nor interesting, is a uniform pine colour, and when the sun finds it, it skips the changing hues and dives straight to a darker, uniform dark brown. They worship Valhalla too. They are made of a deeper blood, and a redder aurora, that's all. They are also faux Egyptian and believe in reincarnation when it benefits them.

Shannon will be eaten by them, and buried in pine skin, instead of a pine coffin and her headstone will be a wooden table. They will mourn her swiftly, by throwing a table cloth busily weaved with funeral flowers over their dining table, in impersonation of the passage of time over a grave, before looking for the next abrupt meal.

*

He was an American cow that talked with his skin,
Whose burger box clothes ended up in a bin.
Wide, padded, shouldered, yellow jacket
Lettuce green acid shirt as they made up the packet
Red trousered legs and cow boy hat
Disappeared, and that was that.

*

Their dark, decorated feet hinted in directions. They wore brown Chinese raffia shoes and brightly coloured thronged sandals as they stood silent on the edge of crowds, staring with their feet. They pointed with their toe nails, which were painted red, and imitated Russian ballet dancers as they alternated feet. Their feet were Africa and Asia, as they took little steps towards their next shaped thought that come from the countries they danced out. They were inspired by a map of the world they think was still secret, it seems.

They sometimes wore fake Greek coin chains over the top of their black balaclava-type head coverings. The coins hung just over their mouths, like golden moustaches, as if they had been caught mid burglary; as if they had no hands, and had dipped their head into the jewellery box instead, like a horse and it's feeding bag. The coins were stuck on with guilty sweat.

They were scared of thumb print identification, people joked.

Shannon's moustache is a light blue black, and is just under the skin beneath her nose. Her veins had to re arrange themselves, to accommodate her uneven features, and the vein, with its faux moustache look, was the result. It looks as if she is silver under her skin, and that it has tarnished. When she is older, the texture above her lips will sag and wrinkle and it will look as if silver coins have faded and sunk in to the flesh, leaving little slots.

While the cult of the block coloured people talk with their feet, the cult of the criminals that impersonate the Chinese stare deeper into them. Both cults are obsessed with the position of their twin skin colour in the world. Cousins are on tiptoe in Asia, and lost, unknown Malaysian relatives sit in China, which is shaped as a heel and ankle. The criminals are only related to them by resembling body parts and not by blood.

They took a microscope to the ankle, and had used what they saw there as their alphabet, in an unbalanced jealous and envious copy of the Chrystian skin, it seemed. The shins of hard workers are stuck on take-away walls. Criss-crossed wrinkles and flea bites, coloured in with hard-to-move dirt, were their inspiration. The feet of the grape pickers and farmers are immortalised as a sweet and sour foil wrapped snack. The crucifixion ankle of Jaesus lives on as a spring roll and chips. Her father's leg ulcer is a setting sun poster, on the wall above.

They are studying to be doctors, they say, as they look at the calendar, and their drawing of the sore. They are jealous of overseas Chinese students who come to visit, and their historical beginnings, and ape to take their place in China, their spiritual home.

Shannon doesn't look Chinese, not yet, and maybe never, so she doesn't need to know anymore for a while. She has not suffered the permanent mumps that some of her genes carry. She may be a puffer fish later and, with her mother's tiny eyes, be mistaken for a boundary baby, but maybe she won't. If she looked Chinese, with darker hair, she will be taught that her feet are above her head, and to look up to people that come from the sole shaped country, or those she know will be meat.

The cow talks with its skin, and she resembles that more, at the moment, like her dad.

The holy cow, and its black and white skin, blurred itself in the mind of the people with it's impersonation of a map. From work beast to god, in one glimpse of a satellite photo, shown on a black and white television.

Hail the new fad, hail to the horned cow. The cowl cult worship with zeal and the cow became their new emblem of intelligence. The cow brought people like her father back into vogue.

Up and down, down and up waves the moods of England, as it discovers its ship-shape land mass. It is going undersea, like the titanic, and the public are echoing tsunami waves as it drowns. They have become extreme in their opinions again.

Her dad had sat cupid-like in the imagined puff of ship steam engine smoke that is their Ireland, as he frowned over his fate. He is liked, he is un-liked, and he is liked. Let me look child: hide yourself away child.

The block-colour cult do not eat cow. The cow is now too spiritual. Its soul hovers over the world in silent contemplation. The cow is too intelligent as it colours its skin to explain its absent, liquid look. They have an affinity with its silent suffering and intelligence, and begin to water their eyes with eye drops. Besides they think they are what they eat, and the cow is too blotchy to consume.

They will displace the cow, after raising its status, and will seek to be worshipped in its place. Every other place has been taken. They will build a house on the cow field instead.

They are another rodent; one that has only seen the dark corners of the mirror. They concentrate on the space that another occupies instead, and jump into it, shedding their cowl skin in favour of dressing what they find there when the light is turned on. They are a cook-you, cook-you, in another's nest, who has always lived here, under the guise of being from a different country. They replace the legal immigrant with themselves.

Sacred cows were another space that they had borrowed, to fill their void.

The nuns and monks, having prior knowledge, had studied cows as they had studied moles, centuries ago. The first chrystian map was the cow skin, stuck on a castle wall, just as she is stuck to the wall of the womb.

Shannon cowers in her hole.

Cows are eaten first, bulls are eaten later. She is more like the bull without horns, with the round cigarette type burns on her eyebrows, she thinks. She is Jaesus reduced to a skinned mammal and a kebab in the block-colour cult world. The kebabs are a tribute to the November sky in shape and colour, when it is raw, looking like an enlarged womb stuck on a stick. The upside down pyramid of meat is rotated until it is cooked grey. It is served in breast-like pita bread caught in adolescent growth over a griddle pan. It is shoved with veiny salad and milky mayonnaise, and the kebab. It is a grey area, where the meat came from.

The food sounds like a slang and shortened pronunciation of 'UK babies', to Shannon. It seems that they have cut the two ends off the words, to make the new one.

She will be food, of one type or another, for them, it seems.

The mole on her fore head would have been a nipple to them. Her head is small enough to call breast. They would have leant forward, in the past, with lips pouted, as if to suck the spot there, when coconuts were fashionable but unreachable. She would have been a blurry rumour, sprung from silent interpretation. Her brains were lobules, fatty tissue, and ducts, floating in cerebral milk, ready to feed them.

They have figural mugs; toby mugs and ugly jugs, to sip from, to remind her, when she is born. They drink at the forehead of the clay cups, that were modelled on nipple heads, like herself, or modelled on fat people looking down at their three-cornered hat-shaped figure of stomach and bulbous hips. The fat became the tri-cornered hats of the portrait mugs.

It is lips and hips that meet in the middle, as they take sips.

It is a spell of childish dimensions. They imbedded instructions a long time ago, on children learning to rhyme and spell, with looks. They wait to see what the adult will do. They are hoping that they will become as trusting as the baby again, as they drink in the simple rhymes, and give them what they ask for.

She is lips, hips, pips, and slips. She will drink, and fall over, without the need of alcohol, while being told she is drinking cider. Their will will be stronger on the abused baby, all grown up.

She has been tin opened around her skull already, in preparation for being made into a mug. That is what the forehead scars are; a complicity to get it over and done with.

Chapter 5

Most of cult people don't talk. That is a universal habit of them all. They are vain and do not wrinkle their mouths for politeness sake. Neither do they think or do. They save their voice for each other, not for the ones they call the animals. When they do use their voice, it is used rarely, for impact. They like to think it is a scarce and valuable commodity when they startle or tease with it. A little is more, they say. They have been like that since the radio had been invented.

They are turning in to pigs and pies
After swallowing their own lies and flies.

There are different herds and they all heard different from each other. They flock together with common colour or common cause.

Some think they are the skull and nose of the UK map and are jawless so can not speak. They are part of the land already, willing to be buried and to be manure. They are copying what they will become next. They are copying a piece of paper.

Everyone is copying someone, or something.

Shannon thinks it is the silent people again, that have changed the nations mood into what it is. They are acting out DVD cloning and USB copies.

We are me, and you is me, is what they hear with their eyes.

*

Cults worry her. Cults and cuts. Her cuts, made by invisible assailants, and cults, with their invisible hold over other people, who are mainly their own family.

It is the vain and vein that hold her thoughts. They have her attention, and that's all they want.

But the Horis knew the truth, they said. Vanity keeps the mouth shut, or slightly open. Not wide enough for words to escape. It is pseudo sexiness to stop communication and to make the mouth look like an anus.

It did not matter how young, old, pretty, handsome or ugly a person was, they said. Neither did it matter if they were clever or stupid. It only mattered that they looked like the last person that they looked like. They were pets, and one pet replaced the same pet, to make the same noises. Better to plan your own future though, they said, else you won't have one. They are impotent in the eyes of the CCTV camera tape that they have watched in preparation of replacing. They do not know how to do anything different, because they were never shown how to. They are sold back the same home and job as their twin had, at a profit to the person selling it to them.

The replacements recognised each other by their ill-fitting and ill-placed warmth, which implied, untruthfully, the shame of doing wrong. They blushed to command, and by practised false modesty. They are Horis. They are aged one or two years old, lied their faces. They wore their guilt like a badge of honour to find each other.

Red, dead, and easily led.

There is so much time and blame in the darkness, that Shannon learns more each time she is woken with the drag of her mothers cigarette. It is the danger and cigarette that keeps her alert and nervous. Her heart pumps with irregular timing, as the hours tick by, by slow minute after slow minute.

She will have to learn to control her blushes, so she will look like one of them, as she sneaks through their lives. They are too strange as they sniff kissed at each others faces, as if they were looking for traces of blood, and had accidentally mistaken the face for genitals and anuses. It was blood lust that sent their lips to cheeks, but they wanted to see as well. Poor people, as their mirror image loomed forward to spy on real age through wrinkles and hair dye. But, as the mirror search the room for pity, like replaces like, and they had done the same to who they had called themselves.

Shannon hits out with tiny little practise punches, in her sleep. Thump, thump, in time to the heart beat. She is there, with them, urging them not to join the circle of forgetfulness, the one that turns them in to animals, with no past that is their own. One story for a thousand faces and they are all the starring part. Some of them group together in multiple delight in finding another the same. They slip easily into each others lives, in and out, out and in, fooling family and friends in alluring secrecy and complaining to each other that no one noticed the deception. They never realise that that is part of their plot; their story.

They herd.

They are a trusting herd, watching the last herd traipse into a lorry, already planning to take their place to a better place.

They were so silent. It is part of the joke, the fun of deception. Accents may vary, even if the looks are the same, so no talking. No one will notice if they have gone. They were one head, and many limbed.

Insects. Many of themselves was the centipede, four made a spider, three made a beetle, two was a flea. They jumped from one group to another. The cult culls itself. It is a countdown to wealth. One can take the place of many, as the foot stamps down on itself. They are six ribbed. Sect ribbed. In Sect ribbed;

wanted for their pin number, which had ensnarled them in the first place. They were under glass and held in place by their bank pins.

She will look when she is born.

She had a story too, though, it seemed, that had tempted and ensnarled her type, in the past. Now she didn't exist, except in one person, who was herself. They had been led to the story of the pyramids, by their own hands, and had disappeared into a mystic end.

The pyramids didn't just draw her type in. The Horis and the Chrystians had been enthralled by them too. They were divided and united by their love of mathematics, and the pyramids were the centre of their habitual musings of their beginnings. The pyramids fitted into the palm of a hand. Both of the palms of the hands have light wrinkles. They are etched 'V's, in the shape of a square, or a squashed diamond. The prints look like pyramids and are thought to be the plans for the pyramids. They are on the palms of all.

Inside the pyramids there are walls, painted with people. The people have outstretched palms that seemingly stick to the walls. Like flies, or spiders. It is an insult, Shannon, or it is a compliment. The people are holding the walls of the pyramids up, but also the walls stay up by leaning on each other because they are the hand.

The insect people are beetles and bugs, with their shiny shell of luminescent blue and yellow hair, and they are the other Shannons, with her same headband head and snaky spot. They are only alive on the wall. Her doppelganger is, who would be herself.

The pyramids are grouped. They look like palm prints in the sand; hoof like, when in the shadow of the sun.

They are symbolic, perhaps, of all the countries of the world, shaped into three dimensional triangles, spaced apart in acres and hectares rather than miles. Most of the countries are shaped like triangles. The pyramids are plans for skyscrapers, some think, and who will occupy them, in each country. They search the skyline with binoculars for rooftop similarity to mummy names and sarcophagus scribblings.

Kick, Shannon, with your feet. Your feet are near the vagina, which is their river Nile of Egypt. Your mother will think you are one of her already, and you will be safe for a while longer. Your gentle footprint there, near the womb, is her pyramid that she hopes will appear on the outside. Her stretch marks are her sand dunes.

The pyramids were all palm and finger talk. The finger tips were little lozenge shapes imprinted on the walls, with tales. They were half as big as the wall bug people. They were lozenges of interest, lined up and waiting to be devoured by her painted twin. Her mentally ill pill, stuck next to her, and its ingredients of bird shit and seed.

She will be a locust, out there, if she is a baby of the block colour cult. She will be hidden under the black cloak of invisibility, disguised as a bosom, or a dog, as they board a plane to the shimmering sky.

A locust, druggy baby, clinging to a lump of grass. She will be a grass hopper. Bony, mini legs spread out as the security guard checks her nappy for brown hashish. She will grow to be a some-time insect. A hoppy, jumpy, skinny thing who will be allowed to sit next to the silent cult, for the way she draws attention away from themselves with her starved appearance. They will prod and poke her for her attention, but really they will be testing to see if she is edible.

They pick off people, from the top, from the high earners, by giving them the same name as the emergency farm workers. They are locust too. They pick, and pick, and pick at them, as if they were at a Chinese street buffet, until the best look like the same druggy scum as themselves. They watch and ape, after the work is done, and step into the tale they have created, or the space they have just made. Dummy people; hoof handed and triple breasted, as if they had suffered leprosy years before, and are incapable of thought or deed.

*

Her parents became tired of staring at the weather and the whether-it-is-army- or- not disguised air ship, and move away, in to the darkness. Shannon's head is squashed, without being touched. There is a circle of ice cold pain on her forehead, and she passes out.

She is in her dreams again, where she is light and free. She flies above the earth, Google icon like, still dipping and diving. She hovers over trees and under heavy clouds. She imagines these to be like the womb. But she is told it isn't. 'The place you are in is made of muscle tissue and full of blood. The trees are twice as tall as your mother, and they are the smallest trees. They have green leaves and are cold. The clouds are too high to touch, and are even colder, but imagine if you want. It does no harm. Reach out, above. Yes, I can imagine the clouds being as soft and warm. Stretch your feet out, and yes, I can imagine walking, softly, along the branches. And when you are born, you will fall down the trunk of a tree, the cervix, like

Alice in Wonderland, passing a library of bleed. I did tell you, didn't I? That's how they speak. Read and bleed. You are lice, A lice, but a poisoned one. Rhyme, mime, and crime. Drink a little of this and shrink, eat a little of this and grow. You are lopsided.

But you want to fly, don't you? Perhaps you could be the dreagon? The dreagon fly, that lives above the sky, made of metal and myra, and everyone will fear er? It's a rocket, and it is shaped like a metal dragon fly. It broadcasts, and protects. It is too old though. It's the president that runs the countries, but it has lost its CPU. I shouldn't tell you, it's a secret. Run old reagon. Ray gun as it tries to bring life to the moon.

It's funny but you look a little bit like a dragon fly. It's the bend in your nose, and your eyes, well, being uneven; they look as if you are turning in flight. You will get lines in your nose, when you get old, and it will look like the spine of one. Then the skin around your eyes will get older and look like the tattered wings of a butterfly instead. But not really. Not convincingly. You still won't be able to fly.'

Shannon smiles, and doesn't care. She is asleep, warm, and tumbling without walking. She is moving like she imagines a flying thing does, again.

*

The country side is in darkness. There is a power cut, and the curfew. There is a paranoid but realistic mood as amateur robot hunters take out their already charged equipment, and set up infra red cameras. Temperature is their favourite subject, as they wonder whether they can disguise themselves to their surroundings, depending on their body heat. Some people wave their arms about, thinking the heat off their arms would appear as distant deers to a machine that can only recognise body heat as photos in the dark.

Her parents think the same, and start to wave their arms about in a stabbing motion, as they walk home. They are their deer antlers. The muscles in her mother's stomach jump up and down as she stokes the air with open fists. It's as sad as Shannon thinking she will be recognised as a cat, when she is born, just because she is the same size as one.

The robot hunters turn on their mobiles, to detect wifi, in the power cut. If they find one, it would mean army or police. They stand ready with their self-written hacking software, knowing it probably wouldn't work, but they have to try. They are stacked against all odds.

The military sweep the area, and unknown to the public and the police, broadcasts a range of frequencies and software while the power is off. The frequencies and software covers every combination and range that could operate a robot and are designed to disarm and render the machines immobile, if they exist, which they do, else the military would know that they didn't.

*

The witches book reads 'Hubble bubble, when there is no oil but rubble, the Wifi switches are in trouble.'.

*

When the power cut is over, some of the LCD screens won't work again, and some computers would have reacted to a time switch, which means that they would have turned themselves off, and will not work again for a few months. Sometimes they will not work again until a year or so has lapsed.

The laptops and LCD's that are switched off by the silent broadcast are important, and the army computer records the part numbers, the software that is installed, and the peripherals details. They could be part of a sequence that could control something else.

Shannon's world is silent for a few days while the laptop and desktop are kicked and replaced. The television blares, but she can't hear it without the computer.

*

When it is Valentines Day, the heart that sits on Shannon's chest skin reaches its final size. She also has one on the back of her shoulder. This is the heart she wears on her sleeve. It is another word game. Which end of her sleeve? The world, once obsessed with hands, is now obsessed with arms.

The arms race was an economical war. The winners are the companies that develop the machinery used in artificial arms, as a commercial product. The artificial arms were to replace lost limbs, and were operated by the smallest computers in the adjoining trunk. She can vision the arm, running around lost and swinging off door knobs, waiting to join the rest of her body by the little red heart buttons she has on her shoulder and chest, as if she was a put together rag doll, made for children to play with. Button A, fits with Button B.

Hand on heart, so you don't break the circuit, amp wire. Vampire.

The arm will pull her out of the womb, with impatience. But no, it will be another criminal pretending to be a part doctor, part beetle by wielding a pair of metal clamps as pincers, trying to persuade the newly born that it is a sophisticated piece of military equipment. The clamps are his placebo arm and are not needed in modern nineteen sixties technology. He would be an old tape of a doctor. He would be standing in doctor space, watched from years before, and smuggled to him while he was a baby himself.

The military has already invented the companies and the varying products they will sell. They have released their inventions at varying stages, and sold them to the highest bidding directors of the companies, who have invested their private money in to their part share enterprise. All are mini computers and phones. They leave it to the publics reasoning to reach the desired conclusion, which is android and humanoids being a reality, and among the human race. The military want to listen and they want to watch. They needed the machines in every home to detect the robots they haven't made, and to spy on criminals. The public will pay for their privilege.

The mobile phones soon become extra arms for the cults. They cling to the name and are insect all by themselves. They stand around, playing with their 'arms', over blocked drains, and getting in the way of emergency workers as they try and find the cause of disgusting smells. They feel at home over the drains, and don't move out of the way when asked too. They are too small to be in the way. It is their joke. As the emergency workers push between them, they are accused of ABH, in the hope that they can sue the government, but instead they are arrested for their beetle impersonation.

*.

Eve reaches for the apple. The apple is Shannon's mole heart, red and ripe. The snake is her bent nose, thorn crown, and white pin point mole.

She is told these stories, she thinks, to let her know that her looks are not new, but very old. That she isn't alone, but she is. That she, or her shape and form, has been documented a million times before. The stories are all different, but they all mean the same.

The hearts had appeared on everyone and everything, in the past. It was Dutch elm disease and Canker rot. Hearts and eyes, all over the place. It was Mer Coeur. The healing sea. The ill in the sea, that makes the heart. It was radiation. It was Jaesus watching over you, Jaesus hearts you, Jaesus loves you It was all, it was nothing.

Hearts and eyes, all over the trees, plants, animals and people as the mesosphere changes. As hot as the womb is, as it cultivates Chlamydia. The atmosphere has a sexually related disease.

*

Shannon was sent into the world clothed

'Valentine' is the word made out of her moles, picked out of her skin like unwanted embroidery. The 'V' on her chest is in the same place as the 'V' on a 'V' necked T-shirt. Valentine loved her. He carved a heart in the V on February 14th (XIV). It is another Horis sum; It is in the second month, and on the fourteenth day that this happens, nine months before the same shaped aurora is seen in the sky. She has its double in her sacred heart, but at the point of its conception. It will grow, as a baby does, into enormous proportions. She has a picture of it, in the mole shape, to carry around with her, as if it was a photo of her own baby between her breasts. It was Valentines baby.

She was not alone with valentine; he had loved lots of women, and had kissed them all, leaving the squashed lip stick marks on the skin. He kissed from the side of his mouth, as if he would be caught, and left a side view lip stick mark on the chest, which is the heart mole again. He sneaked air kisses along the arm too, to the back of the neck, but was caught, and left a half formed kiss there too. And she turned too quickly away from him, and that is why her face wasn't painted properly. Why the photograph is smeared. Why one side of her head is smaller. Underdeveloped, like a photograph is supposed to be. Why her face has been WAP ed.

Sweet stories for ugly people, Shannon thinks, as she dreams. A thousand stories to persuade her to live.

But beautiful people break your soul. They unite, the angelic do, as one. They are stolen and swapped, hurt and made to disappear, but are still standing there, in front of you. When you grow up, Shannon, you will fall in love with one, and then will not be able to find him in a crowd of the same. You will pull at arms, like a mad thing, and search faces for recognition. You will never know what happened to him, and then you will think you see him as a younger double takes his place and acts out his past, and the sadness will break your heart again. And those people, Shannon, are what destroys nations. You will never destroy a nation, and you will never break anyone's heart. There are advantages to being ugly. You will never leave your child or your parent confused to who you are. Your looks inspire trust, not dimness and wariness.

The beautiful and intelligent are flattered into numb obedience, for how could they hurt someone who finds them so beautiful? How could they disappoint their admirers that way? Flattery is the sincerest form of ID theft and trust is built from admiration first.

No one will try that with you. You are unique.

*

Her mother shakes hands.

It is the woman's prerogative to shake hands, in their world.

The Horis are extremists. They add to their arsenal of symbols and signs, and flick from one obsession to another. The hand symbols they claimed as their own first, so they could sweep any history it had into their own beginnings. They want to be recognised as the most revered and the hands used to be all to mankind; the proof of humanity. Hands are the tool and creators of all the things that people are; art, books and machines, clothes, food and fire.

To the Horis the handshake denotes an exchange of what was in the womb, as well as the other meanings the palm print envisages. It is the shape embedded into the palm, that inspires the thought; the open ended vase lines that give the impersonation of the open womb, and of the aurora. All wombs look the same, and they shake hands over the swollen hump of the bent thumb, as it presses on to the back of the hand. Thumb is one, kicking the womb from behind, without touching it.

What was in mine, we will now say was in yours.

When the hands are shook, and not just clasped, it is rhyming slang. It is 'won't let go' that rhymes with 'won't know.'

It is adoption or slave trade, then.

Shannon's deformities have scarred her, but not enough for begging, and she is too ugly for whore dom.

Her mother will still want money though.

Her mother will want money for the ID that she will bring after she is born. The birth certificate, disability allowance, the child allowance money, the procurement of a flat (young mothers

96

with children get preferred treatment. She will be passed around as an extra baby, and that will mean a house instead of a one bed roomed flat.) All that has to be taken into consideration, when money is discussed.

*

The opening of the palm print womb leads to the forefinger and the pattern that makes up the womb shape is a VI. The inside line of the V is the baby.

VI is the number 6, in roman numerals, and the number 6 is the shape of the baby. The baby is called their sixth finger, and is their sweet little 'fing'. Sweet is wheat, which is bread, which is money.

The number six of the palm is used in the beggars and the whores language, for asking for money so they can feed the embryo. It has a head, but is skinny and curled up in the womb. It is a number six. They used the palm to say this number, to indicate pregnancy, or look at the invisible space that an extra thumb would make, to beg.

They say it silently, in mime, as they saw others do, over and over again. Six, sects, sex, sicks, until it becomes a silent 'shit', like the insect noises, as they accidentally use the wrong hand movement in their eagerness to grab attention and money.

When they beg, they cup their hands together to make a bigger palm womb. It used to mean, a long time ago, that they were looking for their mother. It is an appeal to the old. They might give money in case one of them is their forgotten, lost, or kidnapped daughter or son.

Six, sects, sex. It is the number of the beast and the beetle, which is six limbed, and arthropod. They have also become beast as they rush their requests for money, with their cupped,

97

bowled hands. The palms, when they are cupped for begging, are two 'VI' palm prints joined together. The lines that span both palms make an outline of a bull's head, with horns. The number of the beast is six, because that is the amount of limbs the beast is rumoured to have. The two extra limbs are the horns, twisted and stripped of flesh.

They raise their bowled hands, so it is in front of their face and see it as some thing else though. They are insulting themselves by calling it a mirror, and themselves vaginas. They had tried to make the sight a womb to rhyme with 'room'. It seems to be an action of self pity and masochists, though. The wrists are held as if they are tied together. They are beneath the people they are begging from, they say. They have turned themselves upside down, for money. The men have testes that are tits, and grow beards that are pubic. They are 69, the number of the sect, that are sick. The babies are out of one hairy bush in to another, they imply with their beards.

Some of the very old had seen their own squinted eyes and over large false toothy smile in the pattern of the cupped hands and had made small, oriental looking red bowls, to match them. They were narcissus French kissing themselves with red tooth decay printed clay. They were clever in their decoration of the china, and the painted red people were also wrinkled thumbs. They hid meanings in toothy bridges and wrinkled willow cheeks. They had other plans and secrets in their painted patterns too.

Secrecy was a selling point for everything.

The Horis echo and shape their hands into a bowl to beseech the aurora. The two smaller VI's join again, and the aurora is made into an equilateral triangle; an aurora shape. It is a sixty degrees triangle, made from the two six's. They love the numbers. Six is months on each hand, before the aurora appears. Their cupped hands look like half of the globe, marked out with latitude and longtitude. Their fingers are grid lines, and where the hands meet is the meridian line. It runs through the centre of the aurora in-between the palms. Their fingers are countries and hours before, and hours yet to come. They are referring to possessions and time as they count from and past the middle Meridian line.

The hand, in her father's country, Ireland, is used when talking of the animals. The wind is too high to talk and moving their fingers keeps their hands warm. Each part of the hand represents the cow, the pig, or sheep and the four fingers are the legs while the thumb is the tail. The head is left separate from the rest, as they told the head it wouldn't be eaten, and they never lied, they joke. Also, when the two hands are cupped, they can see the same horned bull or cow. The head is in their hands, like their childs head would be. It is too reminiscent to make it a meal.

If she is born, and if she grows older, she will be taught to cry. She will be told to hide her face with both of her hands when she does so, to make a begging bowl with them. It is her bull-face in them, she will be told, and her features were formed from them. She must have cupped her head in the womb and opened her eyes there, to look the way she does. She is what she first saw.

The beggars cannot see the bull shape, in their obsession for pity. They are told though, in warning. Look into your invisible mirror, they say, and see what you will become. Bull and beef, not cunt and count. That is your head, and your legs, arms and breasts are trailing behind you, as your fingers. Take care who you follow home, and who gives you money. They may think they are paying for something else. Sex isn't that interesting to risk their lives for, but they will want to see how easily you spread your legs, and whether you will notice internal bleeding. Death by bleeding does not poison the flesh, unlike drugs, so it is edible. Sex is the excuse for the insane. Notice, beggar, that finger legs are upside down and the head is separate from the body, in meat talk.

The countries inspired the guillotine story, It is a French story, because the seashore of France is a guillotine shape, and the UK is a falling head, rolling off Scandinavia, so not a true story, but it maybe. The truth is lost in parodies. The heads that reputedly rolled out of the father land were not all moles and make up. They were different colours and nationalities. Look at the hair - all ringlets where the hair had been given the name horn so the body could be called beast, and be treated as one.

*

If you are going there, Shannon, to their meaningless world of echoing shadows, you need to know. You are Google flying over morals and ethics. You may be carried to the gypsy fortune teller for selling. She used to wear a fake coin chain around her forehead instead of over her mouth. It indicated that she dealt in Jaesus babies. The coins are Shannon's penny burns, her Jaesus thorns, and bull horns. The gypsies can do nothing but copy what they are about to steal.

They will talk in silence, using their hands and discuss terms. 'When do you need the ID? And where are you going? Here it is, for your own child, for a dual life. See how his face turns out.' But the ID is sold more than once, at a few different towns, and from five people there is one. Cull. Cult.

The blonde and blue eyed are more similar to each other, and they are the baby swapped the most, probably because they are thought to be more attractive and more legal. They can also change their appearance easily, with hair dyes, contacts, and glasses.

Their lives are arranged to the size of the fingers in to sets of similarity. They overlap lives with the same, interlocked finger lives. A five year old may be swapped with a seven year old, if they look like twins.

They are called 'fungi' sometimes, and have bowl hair cuts.

The black haired people are called the dirty fingernails which pick the fungi, the mushrooms, up, or grow them in the dark, where no-one can see them. Some of the children don't know they are in England. There are no official records of them. They are babies stolen from the hospital, or bought from people like her mother.

The faux Chinese are the yellow fingers of a nick a teen addict. The English Russians are hairy fingers.

Their hands move in a blur of explanation. The acrobatic fingered code was taught from birth.

The families who had once used it had recognised themselves from strangers by their dexterity and understanding of their hands, but they were long gone. Culled. Replaced. Scum replaces the soap. They are ugly bestial hands now that hold onto the babies until they turn the green of paper money.

They are hands and feet, that become land and meat.

And the fingers are all the seasons and months, while the thumb is aurora or nothing at all. The people who think they are the fingers of the gods and goddesses arrange themselves in to the year. There are blondes who are spring, red heads that are summer, brunettes that are autumn and black haired that are winter. They are short and tall, reflecting the long and short months their looks pass through. The finger, by itself is three months. A month for each joint.

*

The palm and fingers had touched every part of the world, and was part of every history. Palm print VI's were cut and sewn into every thing. Six, six, six had been everywhere. Turrets, tapestries and table decorations were covered with them. It is the palm print of a working hand, that says how an object was made, by echoing the shape the hand made as the object was made.

She will weave the tapestries herself, with tiny hands, when she is one or two years old. Her small stitches will help her escape and sell for thousands, as she impersonates long dead needle work women. She will thread bird heads, to say the shape her fingers made as she sewed, and her artist name will be the mixtures of the stitches she has used, so other poor people can make the same prettiness. Her hand will grew serpent head muscles, and men will kiss it; they will not know it was once, in eras past, raised to the light in inspection, to make sure the work was her own by the muscles shown there, nor that desperate women showed it to animal type men in penis imitation. They were their own perfect pair; him, nearly on four legs, one raised to hold hers, in imitation of her father's farm

102

hand talk, with bowed body. The hand he raised was the little finger, or the leg furthest away. She was holding his tale she claimed, or rather her own, and naming them genitals, because of the serpent look.

The other decoration on old things is the other palm print, the IXI or M that is seen on an under worked palm.

The IXI, and <u>M</u> s, were sewn into easy tapestries, clothes, edgings, fixtures and architecture. These were machine made, or were easily made by hand, it is thought. It is the 'no baby' hand pattern, and is the hand that means lighter people. It doesn't mean that lighter skinned people didn't work or have babies. It means that the hand is not in the sunlight as much as the other hand. The pyramids, are the same pale hand pattern from above. IXI.

England, a long time in the past, had the IXI 's engraved on doors, so they were not mistaken for baby traffickers, or the Horis. No entry, not believers, no work. No baby for sale, no sex for sale. X means no, and a tick, the elongated 'v' means yes.

Some things were never changed.

*

The European witches advertised their trade with a V shaped hat and a stick held high, that some call a wand. It was VI, upside down, as they looked at the womb in their hand, and mirror the sight with their head. There are invisible points that they surround their heads with, which are used for hand talk. The invisible points are fingers, and their necks are the wrist. The witches own head is the baby's head about to be born. They talk for the baby, and say 'I' instead of the baby, as they plan its life out.

But calm down Shannon, the baby traffickers prefer docile, just as the farmers do, and you will prefer to be sold, after you are born. Your mother is too mentally ill.

The wand is supposed to rhyme with 'hand' but is intended to connect with 'want' as well. When caught, they changed the name of the silent chat to the 'aura', and say they are reading that instead. It is a thinly disguised reference to the Aurora womb, and bleeding, and fools no one but the young, who flock to buy magazines and books on the new trend.

The wand is her dads' single eye brow hair, and the witches swap places as it grows and disappears. They have timed it in the past, once, and it is their secret symbol. They look to the empty space on each others brow to arrange times and dates. They have alibis built, years before the crime.

The witches protest that they are good as well as bad, but they are all the same for you, Shannon. You cannot trust them: the Horis, the silent insects, the rats and mice and the block people cult. The Witches, who are the switches, are all the same. They never move on, and are always the intimate stranger.

Once you are born you may or may not be one of them. It doesn't matter which group they shove you to. The world is all fingers and thumbs. You Shannon are, with your wonky face, a palm, and a hand. Your ears are thumb and little finger, the brow scars are two digits and the middle finger is a bald, round spot on your hairline. It is in the centre. A finger will not grow there, but it will show your genetic intention. Your crooked, mismatched head is a palm.

Hand head.

They will use your looks against you, tempting you into their world with knowledge that you can know already, if you remember.

You won't need to talk to any of them, if you don't want to. No one will expect it with the way you look. You will whisper their terrible secrets without saying a word or making eye contact. They, the good people, will catch a glimpse, and know why you stand by the grotesque; to let their secrets out by being a tableau. They are witch, and you are pointing at them with your forehead spot, which is finger. Witch finder. The bad won't want to know you for long, when they realise.

If the meat traders are offered you first, they will teach you to walk with your chin raised and your nose in the air, so your head looks more hand like. There will be baskets balanced on your head, while other, more normal looking people use their hands. They will give you bracelets too small, and will scold you when they don't fit. They are talking, with things, about how your head become the way it did. They have a story from the 1900's that fits you, and they will push you into that century because of it; her mother has hidden jewels sewn in to the lining of her bat shaped womb. It is the bat coat that Shannon wears as she grows in there. She is a thief going through her mothers' coat, too greedy to search with just two hands, and she tried to grow another one, to grab with. She tried to pull a bracelet over her head, and it stuck there, before breaking it in to bits, that break occasionally through the skin it grew with. If she is evil enough to steal from her mother she can steal for them.

They will give her old clothes to wear to illustrate how well known her thieving is. She will have bat armed jumpers, and

105

bat armed opera coats to insult herself with. They dominate with words instead of wooden clubs. They would climb on her back if they could and give her a trough to eat from, if there was no one to see.

But more history of heart and art, palms and people, because their history may be your future, if the weather doesn't calm down. They will retreat in to the past they have stolen off you, and rediscover customs and cures. They will remember to eat with knives and forks because the bleeding fingers of Jaesus should not touch the mouth. They will re learn that stomach and tongue may become infected by their own blood, and may grow extra holes in their intestines which are ulcers.

Also, if they pick food up with their hands they will be accused of being a retard, that feeds the cunt instead of the mouth: that puts the cunt above everything else. This is because of the bleeding space in between her fingers that they think resembles the vagina. The vagina is cunt, because the finger is used to count. The two are combined to make the insult for people who eat with their hands.

They will make knives and forks for different people and have the features of the person using them entwined in the decoration. They will be personalised, as they used to be, so they do not swap diseases. There will be wide forks for wide mouths, two pronged forks for people with vampire teeth, four pronged forks for four mole faces. There will be trotter forks and claw forks, for those that resembled animals. They will see the imagined scars of the hunting fork in the pattern of wild animals skin, as the animals turn mouldy in front of their eyes, with fungi rings of infectious fur, and will stop eating them when they realise that they will be come infected in turn. They will have to be debased so they can become human again.

In the past, Shannon, they used simple paintings to talk with, while their hands were busy with forks poking the food, and their mouths were chewing. Mostly they had a simple painting of two high fields, and a line of cloud. It was a palm print, exaggerated in to gigantic proportions, and transformed to an outside scene. It was also the underlined eye, the womb and the whipping boy, as it was turned around. Some used the rotations as the seasons and the months. It was also the hours, as it was rotated, using the same invisible fingers to point with. Four fingers to each turn, overlapping at the little fingers and thumb tucked in. That is twelve hours. It was the day, or the whole year, depending on the people's thoughts. They were also family portraits for the finger people, who didn't need their faces painted to know who they were.

One hand was night, one hand was day. One painting was on the left, and one was on the right. The other hand, the other painting, was plainly painted as two mountains, and a lake. Sometimes there were two volcanoes. The volcanoes were an 'M'. 'T' was sometimes seen under the M. This was where the word 'time' come from, it seems. It appeared on a resting hand, half cupped, as if ready for picking tiny cogs up. The Italic T, which is the mathematical pi ^{n} appears in the palm as the action takes place. It is also the shapes the hand makes as it paints.

The diner's eyes flickered from painting to painting as they didn't talk. Their lives were full of secret pacts and passwords, to keep them alive, changing from moment to moment, in their world of easy replacement, especially when they were eating

107

and drinking. They didn't dine with strangers who didn't know their paintings, and where they stood in them.

*

The hand that doesn't do as much work is also female. It is the 'x' meaning no. It reminds people that women that are pregnant shouldn't work. It is the repetitive movement of physical work, which shapes the baby, which might deform it. It is also the sight and fleas of farm animals, anger, fear and the sternness of war that may deform it. Exercise, like running, is not recommended. It is also the chemicals of the pharmacy, of nursing and manufacturing, the water and the land that could harm its growth. It is Jaesus and what the mother sees.

They entered monasteries, in the past, when it was thought that the embryos hear and see more than they should, through their mother's eyes and ears. The nuns wore head coverings that hid the features, in the hope that the baby was born more knowledgeable, and less echoing. It would make them more intelligent, they thought. Echoes and copies never advanced. They stand on the same spot, never wondering, enquiring or evolving. Never inventing. Start as you mean to go on else the prenatal thoughts may come back to haunt the mind, Shannon, and give you fingers too, later in life. They might grow as tumours and grab at passing thoughts, if you don't advance.

108

Chapter 6

Hands together and pray.

There is no form of communication during the service.

It is a place of peace.

There is no show of palms or bent fingers.

The pulpit hides the hands that turn the pages of the bible. There are no distractions as the choir sings hymns, with their hands hidden in long gowns. They are too far away to make eye contact too, and, anyway, their heads are bent to read the hymns from the hymn book. No one talks. The church is designed to combat disturbance.

The confessional box is not for the confessions of the parish, but the wrong doing the parish has seen. The grid hides the confused eyes, the twitching of the hands and darting eyes of the person telling the tale. The priest may be infected with looks otherwise. The priest gives the confessed rhymes to say, to stop them from committing the crime themselves when they remember back in shock. Hands together in prayer to enforce the feeling, and to stop the fist from forming.

Count to ten. Say one Hail Mary, and the urge will pass.

H.M.

It is the palm talk again, and their prints. H M is the two shapes the palm creases in to when there is a slight beckoning of the hand. They are hailing someone.

Hail Mary, full of Grace

The Lord is with thee.

It is also the shapes the little pat makes, that the mother gives to the baby she is carrying on her hip, as the hand bends and straightens. They may know you are a mother by the shape and depth of your palm print. The lines may dig in deeper the longer you carry your child close safe from harm, and leave proof of your concerns there.

But H M, is also volcanoes moving closer together, as the mountains in the palm are squeezed. It is a rhyme said in memory of shattering earth plates, and their frequency. Say ten Hail Marys, then thank the lord that they have survived each shudder. It is an old habit they have re invented, changed to fit the news that is being broadcast as 'live', They count the repeats with the soft poem.

*

The statue of Jaesus used to sit on the left side of the church. The men sat on the left side, to remind them of the danger of the weather.

The statue of Mary and the baby sat on the right side, as to be seen by the women, who may be pregnant. The woman sat on the right. They did not want their child to be blemished by the sight of Jeasus, so avoided looking at it.

The pulpit is on the front and left side, so the sound of the priest's voice is quieter to the women and the babies they may be carrying.

The inclusion of palm talk in the church surroundings encouraged assimilation to the twitchy hand-talkers too. The hands are held in prayer pose, to stop their movement and, because the world is full of criminals, so the appearance of the hands can be noted. Hands show age, and occupation. Impostors in families are detected easier.

The old Psalms themselves are thought to be translations of what the cults were saying, without talking.

The translations were old, and the code had changed with time, but when they had been written they had helped the confused understand the quick movement of the fingers, and the quick look of the eyes that had been forced at them.

Some of the writing had looked alien to those that didn't understand how actions were translated into words. The written words that had described the actions were thought to have followed the movement of the eyes on the face, and the movement of the hands, of the echoing criminals. The former made a curly alphabet similar to Persian and the latter had been more like the straight backed Greek Latin alphabet and like mathematical symbols. It had looked like a mish-mash of languages, and incomprehensible, at a glance, but had been easily understandable.

Rule and divide, as the church was ransacked, hundreds of years in the past.

The raiders picked out similar looking words, and placed them in separate sets, so they could make sense out of them, just as they did with families later.

Look-a-likes, with look-a-likes. A line of a's and a line of b's.

The book had made no sense in their world.

There had been, in the original translation, a symbol that represented the person who they were transcribing, in the same place as an asterisk would have been. A caricature in its simplest form.

Shannon thinks she may have been portrayed as a squashed, lopsided C. with a dot on one side, at the top - A pictorial quotation mark, that opened her silent speech and waving fingers.

There would have been her approximate age, in Horis years, and the time she had spent haunting one place. It had been a normal way of counting for the Chrystians too, hundreds of years ago. 1:10 was twenty two. It would have been to one side of her symbolic written face. Children would have been taught to read the old bible for protection against the people who copied each other, century after century. They would know what time they appeared, what place they appeared at and what they communicated, so they could be avoided.

*

All the clothing in the church was plain. The vicar and the choir still wore white and the congregation wore plain sombre clothes. This was also to calm the congregation.

*

Shannon was a virgin, and would always be one. It was another name for the 'V' on her chest. Verge was the edges coming together or falling apart, always on the verge of bleeding. White clothes, still, for the virgin, who was untouched by the mosquitoes, but bleeds the same anyway.

She was Virgin Mary and the child, all by herself – the VM intials was palm prints, and she had made herself with them.

A veil would have protected her face from fleas, and another human being would have volunteered to watch over her forever, just like the monks and nuns would have done. They would have watched the blood appear from underneath the white material, sealing and unsealing, and would have counted every event while recording the shape of the mark. She would have worn a gold ring on the fourth finger for that, and her husband. It was the dip in between that finger and the little finger that bled, and the ring was to mark where her fingers

113

would have stopped. There by the grace of god, human, and not a beast, even though some said the stigmata there was the bleeding nipple of the beast in her hand. If it was translated in to months, she bled in November. December was first joint on the tallest finger, and November the last joint of the ring finger. She has the Aurora in that bleed.

She is turning what she hears into readable bleeding moments.

She is guessing that in the past, the ring on her finger would have been ruby gold, for the aurora. There would have been garnets for her finger blood, and pearls for her blistered mouth. There would have been thousands of types of ring, for the thousands of types of ailments that people had, and in which month. As she was hand headed, she would have had added earrings to her ear, in self mocking awareness. She would be a pirate.

Her thoughts were living in the past, so she could, with stylish instinct, grab what she needed in the future, without thinking. The world moved fast, as it stood still. Clothes were important too, and she will learn what to wear, by decorating her skin with cloth and colours that showed politics and disfigurements at a distance. They were, or had been, a warning of alliances and of inherited traits. She was nun, with a white band to hide her crown of thorns, and black to hide her trickles of blood. No children for her, as they may be born handicapped. It is better people knew what was fighting in her genes though, so she isn't accused of deception. Two people with the same ailments may give birth to one with less digits, or arms, or legs. She spent all of her time looking at perfection, when she did get pregnant. She would have lived at the nunnery and would have

114

talked to the statues, to let the baby know it has a head to talk with, not just limbs.

The subconscious spurts out at every opportunity for some, and clothes talk for them still. Her mother, she imagined, was wearying a large, loud, plastic gold belt, with a round buckle, when she shook hands over herself. Gold is sold, so she can fill the hole there with food instead. Her clothes are rhyming slang. With the block coloured cult, they imagine themselves medieval princesses, and the fold in the dress is sold.

Her mother would also be wearing a pair of bulging dungarees with deep pockets, printed with daisies and a green leaf pattern, looking like gold coins thrown into hankies, and folded pound notes.

The criminals that broadcast their intentions and thoughts in every way but speech, thought that their silent openness should give them access to others thoughts and things. They could not speak their intentions anymore, because the camera watched and listened. They could not be arrested for a movement of the eyes or hand, nor for their clothing though. They would rifle through personal belongings as they initiated an intimacy that didn't exist, and a bonding that wasn't there.

Shannon, take care out there. One glimpse in their direction, and the victim would be accused of being their closest confidante, of understanding of what they had been asked or what had been implied. They were being obvious, after all. Her mother would have worn a hat, in a shape like a flat cap, with a peak, but bigger than she needs; an urchin, starving style, to hint at skinniness, under the rolls of fat. They are blubber lips, those hats. Fat lips, with no cupids' bow or heart shape in the upper lip and an underdeveloped, tiny, lower lip, with a goatee of head hair.

Or she would have worn a hat of pursed lips - a baseball cap. Peak pulled down over blood shot eyes, and hair covering her ears. See no evil, hear no evil, speak no evil of herself. Her mother's sulky lip hat would be so loud in intent that it would argue for attention with the mouth hats of the traffic wardens, train guards, and the police. Shannon will know, when she sees them, and understand. The police have tall black hats, like they are shouting mouths, with a spittle of light that imitates tonsils, and slithers of moustaches that imitate the hat.

They are who the witches copy, with wand instead of truncheon.

*

The fashion this century is for long hair and large pieces of jewellery, she is told. She can hide her face, at least. The hair floats or slashes in the wind, and turns honey coloured in the sun. It is plaited and rolled, hair sprayed and gelled, and catching bugs like it was sticky flypaper. Oversized jewellery is worn in the form of rings and pendants. The adornments are geometrical in design and computer science inspired. They are designed to be large and concealing, to hide remote cameras and tiny microphones. They are pseudo heavy, made of fake metals, to weight against the winds, but fly in the air. They are fake metals because real metal attracts shocks from the electrical storms, which are becoming more and more frequent. The rain sounds like crackles, in these storms, and is spilt, not sprinkled. Paranoia drips slowly over the population, though, as technology dawns on them, and the fashionable are beaten up and mugged for their mobiles and trainers.

Shannon decides to grow her hair wide, and loud, and roll it in a chignon ear shape, when she grows old, if she grows old. She will spend hours styling it, but never finishing it, like a woman on the TV adverts. She will avoid churches, and sit by cave entrances, listening to echoes, like she is doing now. Churches didn't deserve her looks to disturb them from their peaceful, slumbering, Sunday morning. They sounded sleepy and dreamy, full of common sense and symmetry. Her ear hair will be decorated with white fluffy hair slides, to make it look as if the hair ear is blocked, and that she can't hear.

Haven't heard for them to sell. No herd, hear. She will have show girl ostrich feathers on a head band, also looking like giant cotton buds, and kick her legs so high that from the side she is a nose shape, when frozen in a photo. Her face will match. Her nostrils are ballet slippers, in position one, and leaning, looking for a mirror, while her brows are the graceful dancers arms, bending at the wrists.

A nose stuck in a ballet pose.

She will be an ugly vain child, looking in the mirror again and again, while her mind spins new tales for her to dream of. Her hand face will gently hold its tissue-like hair decorations, as she waits in her mother's place to tell a pitiful tale. She will move through tall towered streets, and her arm will move like a thumb, towards her hand head, as she pretends to check her hair combs. It is a come hither look, a beckoning hand made with her hand head and body. Her hips are an elbow and she will swing them from side to side as she walks, as if her hand head and arm body is cleaning. She will be thrown sideways on the floor, to be a floor washer, if she leans on a wall. They will have her on her knees in literal interpretation, and make her

117

wash stone floors. She will have to dive into dark alleys, so others will know that the hand face before her is dead. Gone into the earth, sleeved and gloved with a shroud.

She will be alive though, arm and armed, with a mobile phone, this century.

Her father's mobile phone, like the laptop, is hidden. The mobile phone rings like a land line phone, far away, hidden under a floor board. Shannon feels the message and nods to herself. She is now nearly fully developed. There is something a little different about her, which is inexplicable. The voice doesn't have an answer for it, like it does for every other slight blemish, and is silent for a while. It is though a sculptor has stepped away from a finished work of art, and has just noticed something astounding, that wasn't made by the artists own hands. It will be a surprise or shock for her parents, and not something they will have seen before. They may not sell her. Perhaps, says the voice, it will save you from the furnace, if you are born too sickly. The doctors may pause, in their dismissal of you, and may want to look at you longer. They will give you clean oxygen so that you can endure the world for a few moments more, if that is the situation. Then you will be like a favoured pet, and be dangled in front of other doctors, and when they get bored of you, it won't matter as you may be big enough to survive on your own. That's if you survive. As soon as she is born, she will attract attention to it. They will not have to cut her open to see it. It is on her head. It is not lumps or bumps, or blood and guts. It is something quite normal but quite strange. It will metamorphosis in front of their eyes, again and again. She will be a cheap magician, doing sad tricks for the trainee physicians. She is the animal that confuses. She is a tree frog and a chameleon, suited to the world she thinks she is going to be born to; a world that has somersaulted its morals into a monstrous parody of sophistication.

*

After the muggings are reported, the hair stays long, but the large jewellery slowly disappears. The hair is now used to hide behind, as eye contact is avoided again. Consumerism attacks with waves of fashion to dismiss fears and worries of crimes. They demand friendship and give beads and trinkets as peace offerings in the lull between wars. No need to worry, see, as civilisation takes two steps backward every century.

The CCTV watches. The cults blab, silently. The block colour cults walk with one person trailing behind two others. They are two hooves and a tail. They are the back half of a devil or a satyr. They have become the hand mirror image that they said they were. Sometimes there is more than one person behind, and then they are many tales and tails, sweeping away and hiding the footsteps of the people in front. They wear thronged flip flops, to show their hoof like intentions. They also like the rhyme the word plants in the head. Thronged and wronged. That is how people know they are native and bilingual, by their clothes.

The front of the animal, which is unaware of being the front, are the other inhabitants of Europe, whose teeth and features resemble various beasts. There are pig nosed, pink faced cherubs and horse jawed, pig ginger Londoners. There are cat faced Scots and dog eyed Irish. The French are gold fish looking as the Irish, and the Russian are wide cheeked pug dogs. Most of them have canine shaped or wonky teeth. The block coloured cult follow them, either in person, or through the internet. They are stalkers, who claim to be the victim. Relief money, collected in Europe for the survivors of the UK hurricanes is going straight to their stomach, which is one of the reasons they call themselves the back half of the animal that is human. Self pity and poverty is the self defence for their deception.

Some of the other cults walk around the towns, travelling from one to the other in thin disguises and used cars. Some wear the clothes of those they have defeated, or imagined they have defeated, like trophies of slaughtered animals. The clothes are worn and used as bait to tempt other victims.

*

The sale of Shannon isn't complete, or settled. Lives are so fragile, that anything could happen before she is born.

*

Shannon's mother is walking through the town gardens that nestle next to the swimming pool. Bird shit is the summer snow, and it settles where it falls. The white, rank splodges make the world look as if it is peeling when no one is looking. The clouds in the sky become more apparent in their metamorphosing and are ominous looking in their innocent cartoon way. A donald duck appears, in a fluffy edged cumulus cloud. A slinky kitten hides in the fold of a Cirrus. Some think the clouded shapes in the sky could be causing the traumatic weather The clouds had been hidden by chimney smoke for too long, and were new again to the observers, who have been taught to blame, rather than to reason. It is the rhyming silence again. They are being told, silently, that the clouds are the same as they have always been, but hear blame instead.

Shannon feels like crying with pity for the quiet do-gooders, who do not know the strife their silence causes, and anger at the ones that do it on purpose.

The clouds fascinate, along with the map.

People rumour, to add interest to their holiday in the UK, that if you looked at a map of the United Kingdom and Ireland, it became America's area fifty one. It is also a UFO flying saucer shape, crashing. They add the five and one together to make six, and say that on the seventh day the gods rested. France is the number seven, or Norway is, depending on what coast is being looked at. The god is snow, and it rests on their mountains.

The alien being studied is England. It is a geology map, in high relief, that is an alien.

The two, twenty five floor tower blocks that edged the town garden were punk roofed, spiky and platinum headed, littered with mobile aerials and satellite dishes that doubled as steel snow and ice. They were the Scandinavian countries too, that also led to heaven which rhymed with seven. Some people, in the past, had been persuaded to jump out of their high windows while they were asleep up there, so the windows had been bolted shut. The people that had persuaded had talked to others while they slept, changing their voices to impersonate loved ones. They were called slags. It was a shortened word made from 'lagging'; Lagging was used in roof top insulations.

They were leap, sleep, and syllable slags.

Empty, glass spice bottles are scattered about the pond, hidden under ever green bushes and left broken by garden seats. Weather beaten men, shocked and stunned through loss, huddle there, reading unbelievable newspapers. Blondes are thick, it announced. Woman re names herself 'Daireah' and tried to sue when people use her name. Mass murderer given lottery money.

*

Shannon nods and sleeps as she is bounced along.

*

In her sleep there are fawn footed black animals, too tall to fit into her dreams, and looking like tree trunks, leaving burger bun hoof print shapes behind them as they prance through her mind. In her dream she looks at the IV in her palm, and it is there. The Aurora, the hora, the four A's which are one, AH,. IA, TA, AP. The fainter letters that surround it are thinner wrinkles and spell PITH. They are the four corners of the pyramid. They are the chrystian compass.

Her other palm was marked by Jaesus. It is in the shape of an 'X', nestled in between the M, in fake old age. Jeasus, kept the company of the whore, and looked down upon the whore. The whore was the MM palm print, given the name Mary Magdalene, clasped with the other hand.

The initials the hands make up are used are used by criminals to let people know what they are. They are easy code and aliases to find targets and friends. PITH is poison. Pith is the skin of the orange and skin of the palms. Palm is harm. The stories hint at poisoned fruit, as two names are wed together.

Shannon is marked by Jaesus, and marked by the Aurora. She is a child of the Chrystians, and a child of the Horis. Anyone would be able to tell, by looking at her palms. She was shamed by her hands. They will be clasped behind her back, or hidden with gloves, so people don't see them, or mistake them for the hands that did the crime. They may do that, when others point out the name of a passing criminal by referring to parts of palm.

Chapter 7

Shannon's mother was wrong about her other children. They were all a product of husband and wife. Of monogamous coupling, as they heard they should be, from the moralistic television.

She was not a nice person, and the children she named plain had wanted to blend in to a background she hardly ever looked at. They would grow and disappear in to another life, one full of baby powder, bouncy carpets and straight haircuts.

They were all her dads' children. Other men's sperm seemed to lose interest in growth, and it would wither away, along with their enthusiasm. Other men were the Horis, and they were casual about sexual intimacy. It was a means to an end. They either received money or favours in return for breeding, animal like, with a woman. The women were either ones targeted, or like her mother, a child reared in superstition and horror, and like himself. The Horis started sexual experience early, and finished late. It was the easiest way of increasing their numbers. Quantity not quality mattered to them. At least one would look like a person who had a job, or like their children, or like someone whose home they could take. Shannon's mother's womb was tired and old. She had given birth to more children than she could remember, and had bullied all of them with a tape like technique, one that had been used on her when she had been in the womb. It was the most reliable way to obedience.

Alcohol, drugs, noise and cigarettes woke the embryo up, and she provided the noise that it listened to. She alternately praised and abused the baby as it was forming, demanding control and obedience, by shouting at a child in front of her. It was repetitive and loud. Every one was shouted at, and, in turn, eventually, everyone would be doing the shouting. It was an ugly circle for the Ori gorie.

Adrenaline flooded blood would speed through the baby, alerting it to danger, but the baby wouldn't be able to respond appropriately. The baby would be born with a stunted attitude. It would not fight back later, if attacked, after being trained not to.

The Horis were a race of thieves and bullies that were also cowards. Unsuspecting pregnant mothers would be told frightening news, something that they were helpless to combat, as an introduction for the baby into the cult. They may not persuade the mother, but would start early with the child.

The television had taken the Horis place. The television had watched, copied, and had stepped into the dark space, in the corner. The pregnant mothers eyes are open wide at the television, instead, and her ears are aware to the slightest noise that may bring danger to her and the baby. Buy germfree, she is told. Cleans germs from the most stubborn of surfaces. Bulk buy.

The Chrystians had fought people with their voices, but they could not compete with the television. The church had sung in choirs, and walked the streets, singing to drown out the cult, and to give hope. Sing high, sing loud, so the baby can hear some good. Seek and replace the time of discontent, and the child grown turns to the window and listens instead of repeating the same. It is a selfish gesture, really, to echo prettiness, so that the masses do not turn their ugliness in to violence towards them later on.

Shannon couldn't hear her mother, or thought she couldn't. She could not hear, because she thinks she only has one ear. She thinks her malformed head, her map, is a medical condition, which she doesn't believe in. She makes up sing song words, to replace the nagging. It is a sing song syndrome to sleep to.

No, Shannon, you are not handicapped, but nearly were. You are luckier than some. You have two ears, two eyes, one nose, and one mouth. Everything that she has heard about herself is an exaggeration. Exaggeration makes better stories, and makes insignificant events remembered. It is laughable, Shannon, how small, how tiny, your blemishes are. They are nothing, but everything. They started wars and divided nations, but united the world too, so forget what I said about your ugliness. Being ugly has a power all by itself.

Your arms, your blemished arms, are the worlds.

There is, on Shannon's right arm, two dot-to-dot letters.

One is an elongated 'S', a single line shaped in dot to dot moles. It is on the upper arm.

Hanging off the centre bottom of the 'S' is a lower cased, tailed 'I'. That lies just beneath the elbow.

Together they are an open mouthed skinny snake, with a poisoned tail. An adder.

The tail sits on the elbow, above the Orion star dot pattern. The Orion star dot pattern sits on and above the wrist.

The open mouth of the snake 'S' is just below the shoulder.

The other arm, her left arm, is dotted with pairs of the same flat moles, as if her snaky arm had sprung across and sunk its teeth into it.

She was the Queen of denial. She was the queen of Egypt, laying in her bath of milky white skin, being bitten by her arm snake.

The SI the moles made were also a cyclone.

A weather pattern.

She was the stormy weather of the heavens, or the heaving's, depending on the accent, as she crooked her elbow.

When it was looked at again, the letters shortened, and entwined, like a Victorian silver engraving.

Reading up from the elbow it was 'JC', the 'J' joined to the 'C' by its top line, and a hook. The Jaesus Crest of Germs.

And Jaesus looked down on Mary Magdalene.

Its formation gave itself a name to be studied with. It was doctors, monks and nuns drawings' that become the alphabet. The letters were 'St' too.

The dot letters were also the ancient, Latin, Irish 'S', with a dot over the top, and the Greek, Coptic question mark backwards.

It is a hammer and scythe, and the Russian flag.

It was also the satanic cross or the Horis cross, as the moles crossed her elbow, where the babies head would be supported.

The word 'satanic' meant 'stain brown'. It was blood stain and question mark rolled into one, as an easy to remember scribble. It was an explanation of her head, as she carried herself in the crook of her own arm.

She was a self taught orphan, who would have to look after herself. Her body would show her where to put the baby, and how to feed.

Bloody Satanists, who would put the baby in that arm, and call themselves her.

Her whole body, with it's accumulation of marks, made up the languages of the world. She had been looked at from different angles; from the north, south, east and west, from under a microscope of gigantic proportions, and her marks noted.

She was Arabic, as seen from the west, Chinese, as seen from the ankles, Russian from the east.

Her ancestors must have been the babies of the two Americas, whose Atlantic womb sits in-between mismatched pelvic hips.

She was equator headed, with Assyrian toes, and as she turned around in their illusion, her feet stretched in to China, while one arm was flung into Russia, and the other arm, with its S.O.S. pattern, was translated by the Peruvians, in to straight headed totems and icons.

In ancient Hebrew, the '.i ' became a numeral, and 666, the number of the beast, herself, with her three sets of dots and dashes. She was a beast when she sweated and run. Ladies walk, beasts make beasts.

She would be, in their medieval eyes, evil. They didn't like human who made beast, and nor did she. She would not run while she was pregnant, to make a crouched creature. She would not make beast, stripped of human rights by a wayward germ, just so she could vainly display her trophy of running strips. Her children would not be called meat, in ancient, long forgotten wars, as they argued of about their humane status.

Her urine would run down her leg, and land in India. Their Africa will be her pubes, should she reach that age.

Her head would have rested in the cranny of New Orleans, and as she reached for the ear that she thought wasn't there, her cyclone arm would have dragged the weather with it, causing hurricanes and heat waves. The original bible was Cyrillic. She was A Cyrillic. She was tinted colouring, a dye, on her face only, but no not really, that was acrylic. The Cyrillic language was a mixture of all. The ancient people's thoughts were transcribed over her. The acrylic type stains were above her eyebrows, on the corners of her forehead. They were two dimensional ears, painted a shade darker than the rest of her skin with melanin tones; another part of her crown of thorns. Ears, not roses, among thorns. She is a May Day girl. SOS, May day, May day, with country flowers entwined in her hair, dancing around Maypoles.

There is yet another story to educate her, and she is beginning to feel confused. There is a thousand images to be friends with, but she will still be alone in the world.

129

It was Midsummer's nights dream and she wakes up in her bower, with love, her chest mole heart, and looking like an ass's head. She is in love with herself. Her fake ears look pinned back and like side long eyes. The bower is the womb, and the man is herself.

Shannon is the cleverer human; She adapts, but no, not enough to be convincing in her impersonations. It is not really an adequate disguise or a startling distraction. She will think herself stupid, when she sees a mirror, that she thought it would be either. It is no protection against the blinded-to-reason hoards. Insults and endearments aimed towards her father's homeland have altered her head. She is cupid, who is quadpid. Four legged and jumping up, rumoured to be eager to please the cold, who are icy with landscape sympathy, as she transforms back to cupid, bearing bow and arrow to chuck at Scotland. She thinks she will look like a dog, or cat, and will be cared for by absent minded old women who have mislaid their own pets, but there is only a hint of animal about her. She may marry a lunatic though, and be replaced by a dog anyway, who would be given her home and her name. The dog would be paraded on a lead, and jokes would have been made of her absence in his world. His friends would have laughed at the block coloured cult looking like the other half of her ghostly presence. Doggy head and the back end of a donkey, when she is dead to the world.

She is paw, so she is poor, so she is por k. The paw is another set of dot moles, three in a line, slightly curved, and one opposite, that is on her face. It is the foundation of the pyramids, marked out in dots. It is the Sphinx claw print, which has reached across the seas and rested its paw on her. It is a cat and dog fight, happening within her body.

The melanin ears that are also eyes are an illusion caused by distance. As the observer moves closer, the outline of the pupils of the eyes appear. They are simplified, and just a shade or two darker in colour than her skin tone. Sphinx hair was the separated colours of her eyes, and her extra eyes might be mistaken for hair.

Some will think the apparition of them is the Holy Ghost, or Valentine, but she thinks that the muscles of her head had relaxed too quickly, perhaps, in a parody of death, before she had begun breathing again. She may have moved, accidentally or instinctively, to save her own life; to give herself oxygen to move the muscles again, if that is what happened.

She has a hero in herself, at least, who saves her life when the dark menacing eyes appeared.

And it is there again, the voice which is herself, explaining to her; the brown stains are the tall dark stranger the gypsy prophesies, which are a threat of death, and not a promise of love. It has been seen in the hand, the gypsy will say, and is already planning the murder of the gullible fool that believes, who has never seen Shannon's look before. They will answer the door to a tall dark stranger, and expect what the gypsy prophesised, but receive the opposite. Hand reading is a test of gullibility.

There is more; She is Romeo and Juliet, poisoned. He is dead, and she is alive. Her veiny lip is the mark of poison. The dagger is in her heart, already. The heart is the sacred heart again. They are the one body, that is herself, and his eyes are wide and stare on her forehead.

The words are pouring in to her, and she cannot stop them. She is reading Shakespeare before she had taken her first breathe and she is turned upside down to hear another story ; tribal followers wore

131

white, and looked for the burning red cross to replace the black one that is in her mole heart. They look like Ku Klux Klan, but are a mixture of all colours. The hunt for the burning cross is symbolic. It is to stop rumours of cannibalism, as the extra mole heart is turned into lips and the embedded cross into a person. They also train the animal of the woods not to attack by brandishing the burning cross in front of them and collect moths on their clothes, to study.

Shannons type was accused of hiding another, secret, stomach though, by other humans. It is another cult that said this. The evidence of their accusations are the accusing darker eyes on her brow. It is the ghost of the victim. The cult claimed to be the relative of the consumed victim who is, they say, showing their displeasure through her skin. Her red skin eyes and moles are the victim breaking through to confess her crimes. They think that her body is dead, and the victim is in control. She has taken a life, and now the dead comes back for revenge, to take hers. Everything that she, or others like her, owned belonged to them, they said. They used persuasion, starvation and bullying for their reasoning. They will talk to her forehead, when they talk to the dead. They will also claim to be with her, when she is alone, because of her patchy two-face. She was possessed and processed, in their cult. Born with nothing, she would have been a slave from birth, paying for her ancestor's crimes, which they said showed through her genes.

She will know which ones they were, or still could be. They picked on the original hand people, because they knew their history. They said they controlled people like her, because of the shape of her head too– she was an extended part of their body, as well as cannibal - a limb made of their spirit, as they decided on slavery. Her cunt count bleeding finger was echoed at the top of her head, they said, hidden by hair, and was their miracle, their joining point. They spiralled

132

their hair up, and dyed it red in conviction on how they made her civilisation by pointing her as their finger, and hand. Shannon will have to bow her head low to show how they taught themselves to walk, when they pointed the bloody finger in another's direction. It is not humility that bends their head, but accusation.

The cult say they are the 'yes', hand of humanity, because of their colour, and that they do all the work, through their spirit controlling other peoples hands. They were the hand in control, the one that was knowledgeable, that the rest of the body followed. They are voodoo, viewed you, you do, zombie makers.

They possess the hand in their rites too, literally. The disembodied hand is pictured in their tribal dances, and held as a trophy and as a direction. They will follow the dance, the weak will, and try the same voodoo with Shannon as their ancestors did with her ancestors. They will profess to have made her point her accusing finger in their direction, as the swimming pool criminals do. It is their first step in changing her mind. They will claim they have taken part control of her hand already by making her point. Her head will follow her hand. Shannon is both, so it will be easier to control her.

When Shannon is born she will look at her palm print. If she points the fingers, as if she is holding a gun, the lines will deepen, and the M becomes a J then a 'A'. When she turns the hand around to point to herself, the wrist will look as if it has been bandaged. Remember that, she is told, because they also use the initials the hand make, even today, in their crimes, as fake identities.

MJA, or JMA., or they use them upside down, VIW. She will know their character by their name. She will know they will falsely accuse her of their crimes, and say they are hurt by her words, as they turn her hand around to accuse herself, or someone alike, of the damage they have done. 'Hurt' is to need bandages, and that is the skin on her wrist. VIW is half of the word that makes voodoo.

Shannon is half hypnotised by the stories, already, but will remember.

Chapter 8

There is another emergency announcement. They are called News flashes. They slip into everyday life, unannounced and unwanted, interrupting gentle family programs. They announce the horrendous with a tapping of white paper, standing it on its edge. Tap Tap. 'A few moments ago the Queen announced a state of emergency,' Tap Tap, ' as it was decided that flood conditions have become too severe for Britain to cope with.' Tap Tap. 'Britain has asked for aid, from Europe, and has been offered aid from Iceland and America. Please keep calm, and do not try to reach loved ones. This is a government warning. The police will have been given the power to use gas guns. The floods have made certain parts of England impassable. Do not try and reach loved ones as this will hinder emergency services. Do not try and phone the government flood lines, as you will not be able to reach them because the phone lines are down. Please do not drive to the hospitals as the roads are impassable.' Tap, Tap. 'I Repeat; A few moments ago the Queen announced a state of emergency.....'
The news flashes finish, and the family program resumes.
A family certificate is given to TV shows that have been deemed, through years of research and experiments, to be fit for family viewing. They are bias free, and are suitable for those of a sensitive disposition, children, and pregnant mothers. They have been standard tested. They are guaranteed not to shock or persuade. The money that is charged for TV licenses is spent on this testing, and insures that no psychological harm will come from watching the program. The program is announced as a repeat, if it is, or if it is a

'live' program, it carries a warning that it is. Repetitive viewing is known to be damaging.

There is also a warning not to sit too close to the TV. A space of a minimum six foot is recommended. A high back chair is also recommended, so that the viewer is not too relaxed while watching, and does not fall asleep while watching. It is imperative the viewer does not take the images that are seen into the subconscious as it has been proven that in sleep that the viewer is as impressionable as the baby.

There are more instructions; please turn off the TV after viewing your program. Do not leave your set unattended. Leave your set to cool down if overheated. Turn off your television if there are warnings of thunder and lightening, as the TV may set alight, and/or, you may receive electric shocks.

The early LCD screens and plasma screens give off too much radiation, and have different warnings. Does not use if your family has a history of eye sight problems or cancers. Consult your doctor, before buying this set, if your family has a history of epilepsy.

The mobile phones have booklets; please keep at least five cm away from your body. Avoid skin contact. Use a headset when ever possible. Affects of long term use have not been documented. Use with care. The booklet warnings are three to four pages long. Manufacturers include the results of experiments on mice, and add the results are not conclusive. They can not be held responsible for any long term ill health problems the user has incurred while owning the phone.

The laptops have the same type of warnings; do not use on the lap or near the body. Find a suitable hard surface to place it on. Leave 5 to ten inches between the body and the laptop. If headaches are incurred check the resolution of the screen. Take a break every thirty five minutes, for ten minutes. Limit the time spent on a laptop. May cause epileptic fits. Consult your doctor if epilepsy runs in the family. Use with care. Disconnect when not in use. Do not touch the screen.

The people who took notice of these warnings pay for their world not to be disrupted. They enjoy an alternative, expensive, reality of relaxation and peace. It is these type of people, who obeyed the rules, that are put into instant shock when they hear the News flashes. They sit, hands shaking, and bowels loosening, at the sound of the announcers voice as it spills over into their everyday viewing. 'We are sorry to have interrupted your viewing. Programs will be resumed in a few moments.' The TV broadcasts the rest of its day time schedule, and years later there may be a break in the mind, where the news flash was. A blur around the edges of normality, and a spillage of unexplained tears, or that is what is predicted from past testing of the same type of people. Sometimes, on the rare occasion it was worse.

The same sorts of families are prepared though. Their front and back doors have sand bags. They have a supply of store cupboard food stuffs and sterilisation water tablets. At least two out of three families have had a member of the family that has served two years national service, and feel safe for a while, until they hear the news flashes. The shock hits them harder than most. They are told it should, because they are decent respectable people.

They have never had rats or squirrels in the roof, because it has been checked regularly for pests. Any lose lagging has been replaced, and planks with holes in have been filled. There are no loose tiles on the roof, as it is checked every three years.

When the wind comes it rips off the slates at ninety miles an hour, which is calm for a hurricane. There is no one to fix it, and no one can be contacted. It is hardly noticed until the rain leaks in and soaks the ceiling. The squirrels, rats and mice take refuge in the warmth, and feed on the soaked stored food. If the people drink water from the attic water tank they will be ill with only a few antibiotics to share. The exposed tank will have the festering corpses of animals in it.

The television will continue blaring, because they took care in where their house was built. They had planning permission for the house because the electricity supply and water pipes were well protected. The plot was positioned to take into account the weather and geological siftings. The TV aerial was fitted by an expert, and is held bizarrely in place, as the roof drops in.

The television alerts them to the danger, and then continues to tell them how to tend their garden.

*

Shannon's leg bruises in sympathy and knowingly. Like it was guessing what happened next, as the water ran down the inside structure of the building, and through the electric wires, that are like her blue veins. The shape of the bruise is like a plug.

It is purple and brown, with tiny red capillaries. It is plug like, as seen from the top, but also like a pair of joke shop vampire teeth. It is a horse shoe, left by a galloping dream of a horse. The horse is a tiny unicorn, and it has raced on her body.

She is urging the normal family that she yearns to be born in to, to unplug the TV, but know they can't hear her, and that they are waiting for another News Flash to interrupt their routine.

Her tiny horse shoe will appear at the same time every year, to remind her to unplug the electrical equipment.

Then it is another story of medieval shields, which is shaped like her heart mole, divided into four parts. The horse shoe print on her thigh is mentioned again, but it is a unicorn. The unicorn leans on the shield with its forelegs. Sometimes it is a coin that it leans on. The coin is her belly button. She is bent over backwards and on the side opposite the unicorn is a deer. The deer is also on hind legs and is an explanation of the sacred heart of the chest as a deer paw print.

Her belly button, in the centre of their shield, shows the world, or the food that is sold and bought. Then the belly button is a coin. The silhouette in the middle was land shaped and shore lined, and then it became the person who was inside the belly – the womb- that grew to rule the buying and selling.

She is Royal and wealthy, but no, she is rail. Rail track as it disappears into the distance as her penny burns become wheels. Medieval is medicinal, but the media can't read, when the pennies turn into millions of pounds. She has been rolled over a barrel, for them, as the belly button became that too.

She is also printer, and printed, between two rollers. Squashed flat as her image is sent to Egypt to hang on pyramid walls.

*

She is sublime to ridiculous, as the hormones flood through her mother's blood, but no, she is centuries of warnings of something, said gently so that there are no panicking hoards hitting past people. She must be a warning, she thinks, to have such celebrity in the past

*

After the announcement, the TV is left on, until the power cut turns it off. Some people leave everything left on, so when the power resumes, they are woken instantly by the impression that the house is alive. It gives them a sense of viewing their lives as others would see it. This is all the newspapers are full of; how others see you, how

139

to impress people on a first meeting. Does your breathe smell? Have you got body odour? The quirky articles are intercepted by photos, just in, of army personnel standing in thigh deep black water, bending over floating bodies. No one has had time to change the running order of the stories. The censorship offices are closed, and no one is in touch with any one else. The newspapers have free reign.

The television echoes the sentiments with the adverts, squeezing their criticism out through three minute slots, of teeth, hair and nails. They nag in between reality shows and news bites. How would your home look to an outsider? What about a quick home make over? A DIY program, perhaps? The News show collapsing buildings and flooding basements. There is an unsaid hint at what has happened.

The watching public leave the electric switched on and wait for the power to resume, to see what impression they will leave, should they die in the mean time, and whether that impression could be improved. They wash up in the dark, and clean mud off dirty shoes. Dirty washing is folded, and they talk in whispers. They were taught the Chrystian way; that others will follow in their foot steps, and that it is better for the community for their foot steps to be clean and tidy ones. They have to agree, because they enjoy meeting acquaintances that are the same.

Their view of the newspapers is that they aren't being ironic but helpful. They do not see black humour or ill intent in what they read. They clean their shoes with care, and, in case they are drowned in e coli, leave them on the top step of the stair case.

The Horis have an angrier way of coping, and are more aggressive. They protect themselves against being robbed, because that is what they would do. They leave a mess to be tripped over, and look with pity on those they know are tidy. They advise, with an annoyance they normally reserve for their naïve children, that it is better to strew the place with possessions, so that would be murderers will be distracted or noisy, before they reach the bedroom.

It is the will of the aurora that the world be wild and bloody, besides, they think they are contrary by nature. They formed in the womb listening to repetitive radio shows that discussed the miracle of splitting the atom and how either half of the atom fights each other with mutual attraction. That is them, they think.

*

The Horis aren't alone, like good people can be. Like attracts like, and they mix with criminals, exchanging information of acquaintances with casual abandonment, with complete strangers. Pointing out the routine of another, as if the person was a piece of nature to be studied, was normal for them. Everything was noted with crime in mind, and they bartered with things like mobile phone, car registration, discarded shopping lists and bank account numbers. It was the only area they were tidy in, and they stored the information with the enthusiasm of new hobbyists.

When they are angry they go to the pub and throw half filled glasses of lager at each other in impersonation of the god thunder Thor. They watch with satisfaction as broken glass and blood mixed.

Most of the Horis have fake degrees in chemistry, physics and biology, all bought from the fake tutors at the college, who are also Horis. It will give them access to wealthier, more influential people, and when they celebrate their new futures, at the end of exam time, they will go to the same places as the more reputable students.

The need to be seen in the right places is relaxed as they congregate in their altered ego, smashing glasses.

They just have to wait for the right time. They have contacts that watch and wait, and others who may spot a twin that may be willing to insect up with one of them. If not willing, there are the Horis women and men who will lie and crawl their way into the home, and once there, never let go. They will infect while whispering their litany of self destruction, in to the unwanted twins ear. They will be mother, father and abuser, who will control. They are the sisters, brothers and cousins within the Horis. The mothers, aunts, uncles and grannies also look for doppelgangers. They scavenge old, forgotten, other people's family photographs or steal new ones. They rifle the homes of the newly dead flood victims for personal mementos, ready to offer their fake condolences, as they sell personal possessions. They will fool relatives into letting them in, while they are upset and stupid.

Shannon would have been forced to be one of these, if her looks were normal. Some children though, just agree and agree, but once they have grown they disappear in to the world of insects only for a blink of an eye. They appear somewhere else with different hair.

If Shannon looked normal she would have changed her hair, like them. She would have had a shoulder bag of wigs, make up and nail varnish. She would have played tennis in a club and swapped lives long enough to catch a plane with someone else's name. Then she would be safe, on the mainland. In a blink of an eye, Shannon thinks, means overnight, on this land mass that is sometimes regarded as a pair of eyes. The mad people in charge have been turning the electricity off and on, she thinks, to wink at the satellite.

She felt around her face with her hand. Her girdled nostrils will be the shape of an ant; one side bigger than the other. She was cat-dog, sniffing creepy-crawlies.

The black ant that is her nostrils becomes the bloated dead, hooked on to the nose that is Ireland, with stomach and chest floating above the limbs, as the newscaster repeats the News Flash at regular intervals and shows the weather map of the two small countries.

'Please do not drive unless it is an emergency. Remember the accidents and emergency services will be busy.'

The Horis, after their drunken violence, will stagger to the hospital, with cuts and bruises, claiming to be hurricane victims, and demand to be seen before genuine cases. There is something deeper than abuse that is wrong with them. They were aping the TV actions that got the most attention. They were acting but they were also taking the place of the people they had watched. Little white mice and drowning rats, still following the tales in front of them.

If there are others like Shannon, she will be the same as the rodent like people: A mouse following her nose, which is an ant, in to a cult, and shoved from one place to another, like other people.

She will get so far in her life, and be forced sideways, upwards or down. She will be pyramided, and contained within a file. Her ant nostrils will become a shiny scarab, as it fills with childish green snot from crying at always leaving. She will be made to battle other dog-cats, and then fed to the lying, so her twin can take her place. The lying sits in England, and has all the comforts of wealth, without working. It has her by her face, leaving a three point claw print there, in pin point freckles. It was the Lion, who were the lying, who were selling ions and atoms.

Europe, the United Kingdom and Ireland is the pyramid that she will live in. The pyramid is bands of countries, separated by sea. The London underground is the burial chamber that she will travel through. There will be Egyptians, clinging to the walls, waiting to double her and double cross her as she blindly does as the last one did. They will rip pockets and cling to passing limbs in the hope of fallen keys and fallen used tissue-like bank notes, screwed up in haste and forgotten.

The map is a simile for a lifestyle. England is normally the centre of the pyramid that cannot reach the top, which is Ireland, and doesn't want to, because being at the top usually means death. It is too vulnerable and exposed. The public jeer, and snarl when it is feeding time, and down with the envied and the worshipped: the wealthy. They are 'offend me', and 'offend me' turns into 'frenzy.' It is a feeding frenzy.

They always sit in the middle, in Britain, waiting for some one else to reach the top, before stripping them of money and possessions. They are the middle men, who are really at the top. The lying that doesn't work for money, and says so with their self given name; middle man is MM, - the under worked hand becomes two under worked hands. Its emblem is a paw, with a shortened middle claw. M and M is also the business man and the whore, hand in hand, in their pyramid building.

Europe is a trapezoid, with the masses crawling over each other to live in England. England is, was, a tiny haven, compared to the rest, no matter how bad the weather was. It was cut off from the bigger danger of doppelganger replacement, before planes and internet bridged the gap between the countries.

The Horis use their arm, crooked in to a pyramid shape, with it's satanic cross, for talking about the two countries and their inhabitants. They talked about it with a look in its direction.

The people and countries they discuss are the baby they cradle. They will feed it poison or not, depending on their mood.

They will discuss politics and economics with the old Cyrillic language of eyes and hands. They will laugh at their cleverness in calling Ireland the top, while conveying it is at the crutch of the

144

elbow. They have made another joke; the dog has short arms; Ireland is dog shaped. It is a paw at the top of Ireland. It is a poor baby, Ireland is.

Her mother blames the baby in front of her while she brain washes the one inside of her. The UK pyramid apex, which is Galway of Ireland, is the imagined poor, that do not exist on paper. The apex disappears with the tides. Shannon's mother holds the baby in the crook of her arm, and says that it will not exist for long. She shouts it cruelly, and Shannon is supposed to obey and abort. She is trying not to learn how to be a ghost, and how to be not there.

On the television, the satanic cross of the elbow is cradling the people who will be named criminals, because they are wealthy. Film stars are reported to have suddenly changed nationality and become Irish. Their children will be left poor, or in the dog. The French wealthy are rumoured to be from Brest, which is at the top of another map pyramid of France, and, in sarcastic bitterness, the good are told that they know Best, in a veiled threat. The wealthy people will feed a country, one way or another. Every country is treated the same, in the media. The television intercepts home News bulletins with News of other countries that have been triangulated and pyramided. The heads and heroes of each country rests in the crook of the arm, and then the heads and heroes are not there. The world is being made in to triangles instead of cogs. When the media reports countries, instead of individuals, it uses the same method. It is Irelands fault, then the triangle will turn, and it is the Scottish, who are at fault, and as it turns again, it is London. The public are in the crook of the elbow, being reaped for wealth. It is the fault of the Swedes, then The Turks, and then the Portuguese. It is the people from New Guinea, South Africa, or Saudi Arabia. It is India, Kazakhstan or Mongolia. And the stack of triangles the News is making grows, and each head has a rest, which is arrest. The pyramid of countries are jarring along, ripping holes in the world as it blames each other. They are the triangles of power that slows the world until it stops.

*

The TV has guided the Horis to use the same imagery as themselves, in a subtle, and perhaps accidental, re- training of their minds. The CCTV records it all, as they talk as if no one can see.

*

The Horis think that the people in control of the television are the same people that built the pyramids, who worshipped the aurora, and the palms of the hands; obsessed with triangles and palm prints, reflections and shadows. The pyramids were built as a tribute to the aurora shape. They were built in the heat and sand as a tribute to its colour. They connected to England in a stretched egg timer formation. The heat ran out of England in to Egypt, in time for its summer.

*

The plug bruise on Shannon's leg changes appearance the next day, and the horse shoe becomes a dark quarter moon. There are two seas to cross, to get from the natural air pyramid of England to the man made pyramids in Egypt. For her it is another anagram, and number game, to keep her amused, while the womb turns in turmoil. It is her moon bruise, twice over, two 'Cs, two X. The X is her palms. She was noughts and crosses. There had been thousands of her, she imagined, all scrambling to get the most wealth and to meet the exclusive all powerful. All following the dream she had been given, and all swapped. All being sent overseas, but not really. They had been conned and twinned, after being seduced with tales of the Orient. CCXX. She had been double crossed, in the past, with a double.

146

From London to Egypt, as the crow flies, it is 3,333 kilometres.

Her doubles had wanted to be free of three. Three was a Horis old age, and a Chrystian thirty six years old.

How tempting the miles would have been, offered by the crow, or the crone, or even the Crown. The word would have changed pronunciation as the con was passed in whispers and looks.

The pyramids sit below the vagina of the Nile. Her half moon sits a quarter of the way down from her vagina and she wonders whether it is a sand dune in their sands, noticeable in ratio and size. It will appear on her leg on August bank holiday and from the time it appears it will be two months and two weeks to the appearance of the red aurora, in November. Ten weeks, or, in Roman numerals, another X.

Perhaps they had called her type queen or queer to tempt her to Egypt and then fed her to the pyramid, to re appear in the aurora back in England. They had a simile in a chain flushing toilet, that has it's tank higher. She had been a queer queen to be wrapped in papyrus, and smuggled out of the country in pretend fame, rather than wrapped in a christening gown. From pauper to perished, as they buried her in turbans, hoping to re sell her back to her homeland as an ancient queen mummy, as they promised she would be. It was reincarnation, of sorts, and she would have had the wealth they had promised, laying about her in museums and old houses. She was their mummy and they are still there in the habits and personality of later generations. She is the thumby mummy, in the pyramid, which is a palm, which is the Horis. She is always lying down in their world. The mummy and the thumby. She was the shadow thumb, but real, hovering over her own palm. She is bound already, in the womb, by her own skin. Her disappearing cuts gave the appearance of bandages unseen.

147

The aurora walked with her, and were her double eyes, they said. They will lead her to her death bed, in Egypt, to be born again in England. The blood will leave her, and travel through the top of the real pyramid, into the unreal one, the aurora, for the rebirth.

It was the story that would have tempted her away, long ago.

They have relations in this country in calling her their mummy still. She was their queen, re incarnated, when they saw another one the same. They spoke to their dead through the living, they said, as they saw her dark eyes, staring at them from the skin on her head, as they told the same tale to entice her. Her looks were spiritualist and medium in their world of easy excitement and enticement. Their belief was the surface of their zombie making. They flatter and cajole, serve, persuade and bully. It is how, they claimed, to have tamed the animals. They are their hands, and had wanted to be hers.

But while she was in vogue, at the first stage of their dominance, charlatans hid henna or red clay, ready to daub their heads with the same markings to fool the gullible into parting with money. They also hid biting bugs in flower head garlands to say they had put the faux liver marks on other heads, and then claimed to be in control of others aging. It was the beady eyed story again, as the petals floated away. It was afro haircut, laden with lice for easy infection and scarred scalps.

Think of that, while you stare at the figure of Chryst, Shannon. Look at the thorn crown and remember their sharp fleas and deceptive smiles. Watch their mood when you are born, because they will be as fickle towards you as they were to your dad, and older generations. You will be worshipped and trodden on, then hung up to dry, like the Jeasus icon is, and wrapped in bandages, because they are ill and greedy. Their hands are hennaed, Hand-head, because of the shape of your head. They know you are coming, through whispers of cycles of the air. They know the pattern of the skies, and what it brings, but not completely or knowledgeably. Their truth is tales told in the dark. It comes from stolen pages, and warped truths, so they know it is nearly time for your type to be born, but not why.

They know to look to the skies for omens, but look past hurricanes and the searing sun. They hunt for apparitions.

Your eyes are there, among their faux embroidery tattoos and fake past, tossed in or shown in their palms as an Egyptian eye. The Egyptian eye has a snake squiggle above it, which is your whitened mole. They caught you in their hand, they said, and pointed at a map of UK again. That is what it was to them, and it was theirs, they claimed. They saw their palm print in its outline, long and slim. You were the Irish baby that they could crush in a whim. They belly danced out your snaky body in darkened taverns, binding and blinding their audience with drugged drink, while claiming to be you, with covered faces and legs, to hide the blemishes they haven't got. They tried again to make a puppet out of you, by saying you were strung up by your moles, but their play on words; their spill on the floor, their spell, rebounded, when they looked in the mirror, and found themselves the darker or lighter mole, grown to full size and cancerous, and that the palm print was a claw.

Viewed you, voodoo, through the CC TV.

*

The white spot on her forehead was precious for them. It was snake, egg and sperm, and their alphabet too. Dot, squiggle, squiggle, dot. Their writing of it, though, reads like a heart monitor, splattered with placenta blood. Or a thief's interpretation of a stolen copper plate.

Some of the squiggles of their written language were turned around, or in a different colour, to mimic another, invisible hand to match her face, or to imply the male talking. The squiggles were eyes to

149

eyes language. Up, down, left, right, back, front, and on they went, with their wish for no mouths, trying to hypnotise with their eyes, by forcing attention towards them. They, like all the others, plotted and planned with the features of her face, as they looked into each others. A more severe group had taken her movements more seriously, and if she had talked or sung she would have been be the working hand. When she was silent she would have been the lighter hand and the other squiggle. Her 'M' print shaped face was a confession of laziness, planned by her spirit, before birth. It was an inert hand, but she would talk, to confuse them.

*

If the writing had stayed in the bible Shannon would know what she wasn't supposed to do when she is born, to avoid the same fate, if the cult still existed. She would not repeat the same as the last.

*

Her bruise, the slithered moon, turns into an eye shape within an evening.

It is a skinny drawn out C and a dot. Give the symbol a mirror, and it is a vagina. It takes two slithers of 'C' moons to make a baby – the waning and the waxing moon, on either side of the nine months. They count with finger joint moons and spaces, and the thumb bend is the ninth month. Thumb, then mum.

The mark is on her thigh, for retards. She has no wish for food or an enquiring stick into her vagina, so it is there a decoy, she thinks.

In the past, men would have been winked at, to show that the woman had its presence on their leg. It was a substitute pair of eyes for some of them; for their own upside down double, their underdeveloped Siamese twin they thought they had.

One eye closed, one open, and apparent to the world. Their secret double wore a cloak of invisibility. It was a wink, and a look to the

150

lips, to let the man know what they thought their vagina was thinking; that it needed feeding. The wink was also shown with the curve of the ankle, and the two together would indicate a vagina, sex and pregnant mounds. Those without the markings would wear a garter, in the hope it would leave an imprint like hers, to fool people that is what they were selling -a look at a leg that could spill secrets – not the contents of their other chin, as they called the womb. She was revered to, in another age, so people could hide behind her appearance. If she had been born back then, she would have been showing her body and marks to break codes, and would have been paid just the same as they did. She would have been a spy and big mouth, as she stood and watched them use her face for a writing pad and her body to entice with, while thinking she was too dumb to understand their language. Her leg eye was also another date or number to make plans with too. She will remember.

*

Egypt is familiar to the UK, in shape. It looks like a spread out, angled version of the coastline of the UK. It matches like a distant shadow or a slow copy cat. This is why, it is thought by the Horis, that the pyramids were built there and why Shannon's types were tempted there.

Their ill matched symmetry produced a face, of sorts, like her own mismatched one. The UK is the fuzzy eyes and nose, Egypt makes the mouth and throat, with its squiggly river. The Malaysian Islands sits behind, waiting to become the ear. Africa is the jaw and hip. The Americas are the skull and spine.

If the air above is full of repetitive overlapping photographs, they wait in the darkness to develop on to the mouldable skin. Whatever captures the sight compacts it into skeletal form through the manipulations of angles and degrees, of heat and gases, and is photos made in to solids. The Chrystians have the development of the camera and the computer to prove it, they think, and the Horis has the aurora as proof.

The Horis say that it is only the aurora that, with the sun, captures the images and fills them with blood. It is no longer a triangle of air in the sky, but a pyramid of one, whose top, which points to earth, makes the self. Its four sides capture the fours sides of the world, and combine it to make one half of the human, animal and insect, as all images combine to peter out to one image.

And when the moon illuminates the aurora, from another angle, it makes a photograph for the other half of them all, and forms the bone.

*

The Horis are still full of the atlas as they think these things. They think with thoughts that have been planted, but are not aware of it.

England and Ireland is now also the paw of the household cat. It is the way the earth turns that changes the view. This means Egypt's coast is the paw of England and Ireland, dragged out. It is the paw of the tiger, the lion, and the panther. The sphinx was built, some say, to show how large the cat would have to grow, to fit their theory of ratio and gigantism. But the sphinx is a stone elephant whose nose has been broken, and the camel is walking lips, so the transfiguration is believable. There may be angels, cupids and pegasi, out there, in distant galaxies, who have been shaped by the world too.

The public want to believe it is true and in the heat and drought begin to think it is. Stories circulate and sightings are recorded of winged creatures, thought to have existed only in the past, when the world was new and the air was thin enough to reflect back on itself, to make them. They have mirages, the TV and melted airwaves to help them with their imagination. They also have a devotee in the

TV, to dictate the nature programmes, who sorts species into countries which match their shape.

When the sky changes, the appearance caused by transfiguration changes, they think. The hurricanes sweep the skies, churning and confusing the atom air, and change the photo that is developing in it into something else, to be reflected in to space, to make the winged creatures. The angles overlap, making their angels flap.

They know it is true, they say, because of the change the hurricanes make on the appearance of humans, at the same time. The inverted pentagram with its centre of a goat is a symbol of this. It is two triangles overlapping, that gives two photos to the genes, that gives the goat twice the length of lips and teeth, and two times the holes it needs for eyes. They are wings, in another dimension, and the goat changes to horse, to fit the ratio.

The inverted pentagram was used as a weather symbol that meant the islands - England, Scotland and Wales - were surrounded by hurricane weather, and that the air was ready to be sucked in and spat out.

The photo would change.

The windy air had sharpened in to deadly points. It meant isolation for the islands. The goats in the centre symbolised the hurricane shape too, in its spiral horns. The horns were penny brow burns, built upon penny brow burns- holes upon holes. The goats were wealthy in pennies. They were Scrooge counting the pennies piling up about their ears, and looking down at their half fingers. The wind will come and whip the skulls of humans into the same shape, as the massive become the miniature. It lived in the water, the shape shifter did, or the air, and come with pollution. The water had spit and scum in it and wasn't drinkable. The children born of it may be misshapen or deformed, as the brain fought with the genes at the picture they

153

were staring at, they said. Her eye stains were wings, in the wrong place, and the penny burns were bones of feathers. She was upside down here, in this upside down country, waiting to be born the right way up.

*

The emergency farm workers miss their showers when they see the symbol scrawled on to a piece of A4 paper, wrapped in plastic and pinned to the door, and go to the swimming pool to clean themselves instead. Some of them, the hidden Horis among them, who were there to watch, think it means they are going to be paid, secretly, without the others knowing and sneak back to the showers. The inverted goatee pentagram, to them, was as a handshake with money in between. The two triangles are palms. When no money or boss is found, they use the showers anyway. The water seems normal, but soon phlems out unseen dirt, as they clean themselves. It mingles with their own muddy skin.

*

There are more handshakes and money in the air. The hurricanes have landed on the islands with determination and heat and it is seen, by the Horis, that the hands of the world, of the countries, of the air, are clasping each other and that the pyramids are crossing over. The pyramids are in the UK, delivered in clay dust and gorging flies. The aurora is in Egypt, in the form of the sun, doubly heating and turning the swelling vaginal Nile red with baked sand.

The two countries swap more; they swap diseases and tinned food stuff, as Egypt lands in the United Kingdom. The air is spitting its forge blast warmth in every direction and the landing planes are full of dark strangers with thick black moustaches. Frogs turn into lizards, and Norfolk grass snakes develop poisonous patterns in the heat.

154

The mystics and the spirituals are spellbound by the weather. They buy charms, more henna, take up yoga and chant. They came to England to see this, and to make money. It is, the spiritual think, the red air becoming earth, and becoming Egypt as Egypt becomes the red air. It is a result of years of incarnations. Long dead bodies and gold trinkets will spill up from fractured roads and ghostly wind patterns will lurk in the sky. They hope the judges will believe this if they say it for long enough, with enough conviction, when they are caught with stolen stuff.

More churches are burgled and icons are covered in graffiti with a surge of anarchic belief, while panic buying causes a food shortage. Some of the TV viewing audience buy long shorts, in army grey green, and wear cowboy hats, as if they are in an adventure film, treasure hunting. They leap on anything sparkly, and run off with handbags. The world is sodden with conflict and loonies, competing for attention. Insanity is fashionable and they all have food poisoning.

Her mother suffers with them all. She sews red triangles, for aurora flag waving, and eats rotten eggs. She slips on a disguised personality for the church, and lets a few tears develop when she sees the broken organs. Church is a place where she has to be careful. She cannot show herself to the enemy, so she cannot show herself to friend either.

Shannon feels broken herself. There had been another change in her appearance. The question mark moles that are on her arm repeats itself under her chin, and down her neck as if it has just noticed her head is another hand. It looks like the meat hooks of gangsters, hanging around her throat or the hangman tarot card.

She is worried about serious people who would think it was an instruction for murder. They may have pyramided, her distant cousins may have been, by others thinking they had been instructed to do so by the dot-to-dot skin pattern. Logical computer thought is the norm for some people. They were self robot styled and emotion free, and the moles looked like dress pattern instructions.

She is a cracked mirror, and a pizza head, cut in to fours and put back together again, to confuse them. The question mark around her neck is a pizza slicer. It is an actor's scythe. A hook, under her chin is ready to pull her off the stage. It is also a big ear, and the big question that she can't spit out, stuck in her throat when she is faced by machine that is human, and human that thinks it is machine.

Chapter 9

The town that Shannon is developing in is on the grid line that lies thirteen degrees west of Greenwich. She is inside a thirteen, inside another thirteen, which is the UK and Ireland. The UK is the three, and Ireland is the one. Her mother, she thinks, must be a thirteen too. It was thirteen, thirteen, thirteen everywhere, for a while.
Unlucky 13, Britain, when the winds hit.
 She imagines her mother as a straight back and a two bulge impersonation of the countries. She is a Russian doll inside a Russian doll, just as the world seems to be. The number was analysed and computed to connect to the UK's other shape; the one of the growing embryo.
$3 / 1 = 1.5, 1.5 / 2 = 0.85$
The resulting number is nearly nine months, and number threes are written with bulgy bottoms to show that pregnancy is hidden within its lines. $1+1 = 3$, and Ireland is an Italic one.
Her mother must be wealthy, Shannon thinks, to be able to give birth in a country that emulates the number and birth so precisely.
But she is imagining the past, where Beth is Birth, and is the queen of the economy and of tourism. The islands had been home to intellect and to laziness, for the pregnant, and about to be born.
It isn't true anymore, but she is here, growing in the holiest land of the Chrystians, in the most worshipped of Horis places, long after the sightseers were all gone.
She knows, but doesn't know how she knows, that the town she is in had been bombed, knocked down, and replaced by modern buildings. Its history had been hidden and forbidden, for one reason or another.
The town had been re-built to echo England. That was why her father had moved to the town, to build, many years before.

The centre is a little London, fashioned as if it was a toy train town or an arch criminal's master plan mock up. The town clock is a miniature of a stripped version of Big Ben. The metal supports and a blank face sit in a square of a water pool, as if Westminster had sunk into the Thames and had survived as scrap value.

The pool of water is edged in black marble, as if in mourning of this fact, and a water fountain impersonates the grey spires of Westminster, just as Westminster impersonated the grey spires of water fountains.

Its surrounding shopping area, although it looked fairly ordinary, was planned according to the layout of an older London, with the well known accentuated as shops. There was one butcher shop that was placed as if it were Spitalfields Market, east of the clock. There was a small theatre, across a bridge, in an impersonation of Shakespeare's Globe. There were parks placed about that represented the Royal Parks.

One common ground garden pond is in the shape of a water bottle, or a gun powder sack. It lies just outside of the town. It also represents England and Scotland in its shape. A tiny bridge crosses where the lid would fit, and where the Hadrian's wall would be.

The pond is in the swimming pool park, with its spicy garden and Norwegian tower buildings which doubles as a studded belt. The water bottle pond is casually slung into the landscape with a grey winding path that is a pocket.

The designers expanded on the idea of the water bottle with linking the pond to an underpass on the never ending road. The road is the leg and pocket of the trousers. The roads are grey, like the sea. It is a hint of an underground tunnel to Ireland. The swimming pool is a shiny debit card case, which will pay for itself.

159

Further away, her parents' home sits in a square cul-de-sac, on the corner, or the centre, depending on who is interpreting. There is a path along the centre of the cul-de-sac. At one end is an alley that leads to a long road, and the other end is open. The alley isn't designed to be seen from above, and is covered with cherry blossom. The other open end is a semi circle, with a white blossom tree in the centre. It is, altogether, the illusion of a full champagne glass, with the white blossom acting as fizz. The cherry blossom, which is deep pink, as it lines the alley, looks like the stem of the glass as it is seen through a sun set. The square cul-de-sac sits in the back ground, like a bordered menu, propped against it.

Above the champagne glass is another arrangement of houses. These have a low fenced alley with deep red rose bushes either side that make it difficult to walk through. At the end of the prickly path there is a cocktail glass shape to the pavements as they sharply divide to make two sides of a street, and the top. These are retirement bungalows and a triangle cul-de-sac. To one side another road leads in, looking like a cocktail stick, with a round of deep red bushes sitting to one side; they are the cherry on the end of the stick. It was an investment story and a romantic tale. It is a hushed dinner, with two glasses, and a conversation that is wondered at.

It is Europe as a person, and it's a dropped bottle that is the United Kingdom. She was living in a wine bottle label.

There were more designs hidden in the housing, and more echoes of the capitals of the world set along the line running thirteen degrees west of the Greenwich Meridian. The next town emphasised a Germanic influence, in it's architecture and planning. The town next to it had the gardens of Paris lain out in miniature. Peterborough had its Russian influence, in name and designs. At Hull there was the Deep aquarium, with its Australian opera house type design.

Brighton, at the other end, had the Royal Pavilion, emphasising the onion roofs of the Orient. It was the circumference of the world, shrunk to the shore lines, for pregnant women visiting from abroad, with all the buildings intact. Only the town she was growing in had been destroyed, along with parts of London.

The towns were a sight-seeing tour for those who could not travel off the islands too, before shipping and flying was a normal pastime. It was a grand mini tour of the eighteen hundreds, built by the ruler, and the ruler was twelve inches long, with Ireland as a one added, that made the same thirteen. England was at the beginning of the bio computer world. The ruler was a computer and it was built by binary, in ones and twos. The clouds over England were also binary. Lines and circles, like her arm.

*

Her mother had waved goodbye after she had spoken to the meat woman.

It was another type of secret handshake for her, but was a common knowledge secret for all. It was a sign of knowing about the longtitude and latitude of the town, and the special placements of its features, of knowing it was doubly special for being a little double of England's capital.

It meant you had a computer and knew where to look. The wave had been handed down from past surveyors and switchboard operators, who were the old privileged.

Four fingers, waved three times, and then the thumb. It meant 'see you in the town.'

Later the Horis will be giving each other high fives, and slapping down the hand offered to them. It is actions instead of words. Together the actions spell 'sla- and- hurt', 'slandered'. They bite the

161

hands that feed them, or near enough. They hit and thump arms instead of mobile phones.

*

Shannon was a high brow. High brow. He brow Hebrew. It was a matter of accents and accentuations in their world. She was an eye brow. They knew about her eye brow scars, she thought. She had been pre-destined again, before her birth. Shannon's Shakespeare shadow ears looked as if they were pinned back to her forehead. She was listening with her animal sixth sense, they would have said. They were positioned as if she were sprinting forward, splitting the womb in haste as she escaped. They were her surprise to the world. She would not be Hebrew either. One side, on even closer inspection, was in the shape of a face, cringing. It was a crude portrait of her own lop-sided face. The other melamine ear was a scull. She was coin head.

The tiny portrait was not usual.

It will appear with sunglasses, when it gets too hot. If it gets very hot a cigarette shape will also appear, hanging from the pseudo mouth, with a bright red spot under the pretend lip of the mini face. As if to emphasise its point, another red spot will materialise under her normal lips. It was a gif to fool the machines; androids and robots. It was a simple diagram pictogram. It was a power point presentation. The mother smoking will harm the baby. Do not smoke. The baby is witch already, changed in hue by cigarette smoke, and the mysticism that surrounded her father.

She has a public health warning on her forehead. Her faces will stop her agitators in amazement and horror. She will be adopted by a maker of weather clocks, and turn each side of her face, depending on the weather. The melamine eye skull side, which is on the bigger, bulgy side of her head, will be starving and flooding, and the other,

162

too much heat. She will live in a bed, and never get out, but turn and twist her weather announcements to the world.

She is a miracle.

She will be born blessed with an intelligence unknown, that is new or forgotten. Her appearance in the world will bring the proof of the existence of God, and bring peace to the spiritually starved islands. The populace will turn to the church, instead of fighting, and find peace and a community. They will rebuild fallen walls, and nurse each other through windswept horror. She will wear white and have a crown made to cover her own crown. It will exaggerate her marks, so even those that can not get near will know of her status in the world. She is queen again. They will see from a distance her superiority of her skin, born of a mixture of all races. They will love each other again. She will have a nursery of silver and gold play things, and only drink fruit juice and water. An engineer will make her a pair of wings, and she will fly every where in a daze of beauty.

But she would be shot down. Others would not care about her other face. She would be just a flying thing guarding their treasure for them, just like other babies probably had been, whose parents had been tempted in to the islands to give birth, by its shape and distance from earth bound enemies. Her wings would be given to the next heiress, for the span of her life, which would be as short as hers.

She would be a dragon as she fell, because next she was their snake, which they claimed to have hypnotised out of a basket. It was transfiguration again that divided and changed her shape, as it divided air mass with angles, as she dropped to the earth.

The persecutors have a whistle, and like attracts like, they say, as they look at her cigarette burn scars and her shadow eyes before blowing into their pipe. They hated her, as they tried to be her. It is the sight of her, in the past, that showed the possibility, of having lighter skin, which never came true, that make them refer to her in their tales. They would have drained the blood from her arm and drunk it in small vials to change their colour. They are what they drink, they thought. She is hated for broken promises that she never made. Their pigmentation never changed. They would have drained her Orion arm, the one they thought belonged to the night because of its appearance, and would have waited for the slow change in their own skin. They would have nodded at her other arm, with its fang bite shapes, to say she gave her consent by her appearance. They had been conned with it for eons, with lying hennaed tales about her powers of change.

To some she is Kali. She is a deity. She has many arms they heard, to match her many faces, but they heard wrong. That is the weather map of the world, and its arctic arms of winds, waving over the continents. In their world, she has six arms. They are the muscles and bone of the arm, separated and left to float in the wind, as they over bloodied them. Biceps, triceps and humerus looking as if they are carrying the tools that made them that way, so they could say she did it herself. It was voodoo, fooled you. If they said it often enough, they would become whiter that way instead, by tricking the eyes with the mind. They would have swallowed the small skin heart mole as a delicacy, as a way to change their own heart. Her statue skin is blue because it is all veins. They have sucked her arteries dry. Her matching blue tongue is more rhyming slang- she is 'you young', for their aged, darker skin.

Their Kali is her, but isn't. The name Kali is Irish. It is a sea weed. It takes its name from California, or California takes its name from seaweed. Both are underwater, as the sea soaks the world. The comparison is quick and easy, as the computer shrunk world is seen and heard, within a few minutes, over the internet connection.

*

From the top window of the house that her mother and father rents there is a view of the cocktail glass cul-de-sac, partially obscured by the white blossom tree. The internet chat room gossips about the residents, of their income and their morals. Like attracts like, and they hope they are. The large shaped street is too ominous to be ignored. It is triangle shaped. Do they meet on the corners of it, they type to each other. Is their centre, the corner? One resident appears in her garden, as she hears others walk past. Her bungalow is in the centre of one side of the street, and seems to be one point of a pentagram. They have a code perhaps, because if they see the same person twice, another person appears on another point of it. They, one of the gossips transmits, always has a watering can that is silently filled. There is no dripping tap, or squeaky pipes. No water appears in the drains, yet it is always full. There is a water shortage. They are not allowed to water their gardens, in the drought.
But it is any petty excuse to persecute.
It is a switch hunt. They are looking for someone they can switch with, under the cover of righteousness, and this time the switch is a tap.

*

Tap. Tap Tap, Same drivel, just a different way of saying it.
Shannon listens, already bored of their triangles and stars, but she wants to know whether she will be slid in to their other drinking glass street, like a dash of lemonade or gin.
Perhaps they were poured from one to the other, using dead identities. Or perhaps she will drop out of the womb, unnoticed, and blow and bounce about in the hurricane wind, waiting for

165

recognition. She is a goddess, of sorts, after all. The wind will be her wings. The boughs will bow in her presence and leaves will soften her falls. She will fly above houses, with the grace of an angel and the figure of a cupid. She didn't mind. She just wanted to be free of the mold she was in. It was a mould of cold, and she was going to be sold, and never grow old

*

They are typing in code. They like code. It gives them a sense of intelligence and of self importance. They are being secretive, even towards each other. They type with a fast, humped back, way, like the Scrooge they have seen on the telly; fingers grabbing and poking, and ash from fags scattering the keys. They are, it seems, plotting what they would do if they moved into the cocktail glass. It is a prized position, within the town, but no one can say it out loud.

They put the fear of death into the back of their mind. They have never asked what happens to the people who they replace in the world. Why they have a job, when there are no jobs. Why they can buy a house a third of its value. They know that they are involved in witch craft, switch craft, and that the people they are replacing are probably dead, but they never worry about themselves dying early.

It does not happen to them, they say to each other.

They rely on the unspoken truce, they think, that criminals have for each other. They do not think that others relied on the same misplaced trust. They bond with each other by using the guilt of bad mothers and lost babies. They are each others baby, and stare wide eyed and trusting at each other, each holding a weapon behind their backs. To show open envy is to be the accused, when the envied disappear.

The television and the internet have tried to make witchcraft glamorous and fun. They have tried to take the place of the church and have tried to assimilate cults. They advertise ghoulish clothes and play horror films late at night as they assimilate to alienate. The films are advertised as not being suitable for pregnant women, but being bad to your self is fashionable now, according to the same source. They advertise it in the breaks. Shock tactics to make them buy. Eyes are opened wide and it's the ice cream trolley in the aisle. I scream, and ice cream. They eat the sound they make.

*

Most of the women who are switch craft seem ugly. They have a cultivated look of plainness, bought on by over eating and laziness. They try to seem as if they are not interested in the world, when they are constantly staring at it. Their lives are adrenaline laden, and they watch telly with a blank stare and view their own lives with the same blank stare. They can not help it, they say, they were passed from parent to the machine, and the machine was in agreement with wrong morals.

Everyone is becoming the same ethics though, even the ones with good parents, who obeyed the laws and rules, are being re created in a roller coaster of chemicals and contrasting TV. They are learning their behaviour through the wall of the womb and prepare themselves for the outside world, and adapt to the majority. The TV is dictating. It is the loudest. Before the TV it was war. Before the war, it was the cults.

The people are trained. Good doggy people. Have a sweet biscuit.

The TV schizophrenics - the switch off, switch on people - live in a world where no one gets any older, and no one dies, even after they are dead. They understand why their children never grow up, and can not see any change in their own age, when they look in the mirror.

Shannon is prepared for this threat and the TV pensioners, who stare over their evening drinks while reading the financial times, who apparently live in the cocktail glass road, and are worse. They keep their laptops in slide out draws, and use the web cam to record visitors and passer-by's. They look at her mothers street as if it was a stemmed glass of cheap lager, with plastic ice cube cars and a dirty, blood stained stem. The road between is a welcome sheet of glass, especially in winter, that separates the streets. When the rubbish is put out for the bin men, they are, to these people, like fag burns on a bleached white Formica table. Their own rubbish is left to the last minute, to fit their idea of what is proper and fitting, and to stop people rifling through it.

It is tied at the top, in to neat little bows and sprayed with room spray. The bin men have to pick up the rubbish there, after visiting a little row of shops that sits a couple of streets away. They stop to buy the paper, and to pick up assorted rubbish, they gossip. The butchers shop never stop shocking the bin men, with their assortment of bones, rotting meat and maggots, and there is normally a hole in the rubbish bags where the rats have chewed through, but since the hurricanes have worsened, they have been blown everywhere, and it is more like a battle field scene that they have to clean up. Most of the town is like this.

The bin men drive to the cocktail glass street and arrive with a look of astonishment on finding the street abnormally clean and tidy, as always, while everywhere else is dirty.

The perfumed rubbish bags, with the tidy bow knotted tops, eventually make them physically shake with nervous anxiety. The residents are just too odd to feel comfortable with, and the bin men regularly check the bags for human bones by feeling through the sacks with muffled gloved fingers, they type.

So they might be the same.

Shannon imagines her father is the same as the bin men, as he touches her mother, feeling her warily for hidden baby ribs, and pieces of dead cat, wondering if anything else has been perfumed with cheap toothpaste and hidden in her folds of fat.

*

Of course, not all the people in the world are cult, but she doesn't know of the normal people. She is only told of the small big world that she will be born in.

*

One plus three is four, which rhymes with whore.

Like the Kali cult that will claim that California is theirs because of a slight arrangement of words, Horis claimed that the thirteen towns along the west 13 belong to them because of the rhyme. It is their play on words again, as they scribble the numbers on the floor with chalk, and jump up on down on them. Ownership papers do not matter to them, as they will have the same fate.

The thirteen countries that the towns represent are theirs too. They are the matchbox sellers that think they own the factory, because they know how to make a match.

They spend hours pouring over maps and measurements. Ratios and ruins are studied. They are sure they have found a hidden Egypt, and for a few hours Shannon is interested in being part of their pyramid of living. They convert the landmarks of England in to inches, and try to fit the ratio into to a standard twelve inch ruler. They try to find the invisible inch. They are sure the two are connected.

Brighton to Scarborough, as the crow flies, is squashed.

It is 400 kilometres, or two hundred and forty eight miles. They divide the 400 kilometres into 12, and are amazed at the infinity it shows. One inch is 33.333 kilometres recurring. That is their invisible measurement. Infinity.

169

They swing the ruler around, and compare it with the coast line of Egypt and Libya.

They are still wearing the long shorts of their imagined Sahara, as they try and think of the opposite number of 3, as they think it is the equivalent of tree and Egypt is the opposite to England.

Can't see the world, for the threes.

What's the number for sand, and they think of hand.

A three to five ratio, is the answer to their puzzle, and the chat-rooms are full of self congratulations as they stretch out England to fit into the Egyptian coastline.

Mathematicians and unseen angles are in the feature part of the newspapers. They are admired and held in awe. They can measure the speed of light, and the way the atoms are expected to travel through it. They talk of dark light, and magnified angles. The way large bodies of water refracts and reflects is the topic of the week, as a headline of the tsunami floats above it.

It would be a hand, they agree, because of the pyramid, and because of the Oris, as they affectionately call the aurora. They are overjoyed when they calculate the answer as 666.66 kilometres and it fits the shoreline border of Egypt. It does not matter to them that they have not explored all the possibilities of connection; in fact, they have just pursued a convenient path.

They were 'reared' by the TV, and the quick, easy to find conclusions of adventure films. It is all over by the TV commercial break, and they reach for something to consume with their spare hand. Even as they type, the kettle is being heated for tea making, as told to do so by the telly.

*

The ratio, even though it is correct for the Egyptian borders, does not include Libya. Libya has a hump of land similar to Norfolk, and would be included in the four hundred mile zone. Also, it is the coastline, not the equivalent of where the line of British towns lay, which would be inland. They have not noticed, and are full of self praise. Shannon falls asleep as they share a bottle of wine and vodka. She is calculating what she would do if she were on the other side of the womb. She would find where the sky scraper towers would be, using the same ratios, and find the people who are in control.

*

The statue of Jaesus raises open hands to the skies, as eyes look upwards and inwards. The palms hold infinity within their pyramid prints.

Jaesus is never ending.

One begets another, who begets another, who begets another, into eternity. Thoughts are infinite and the eyes look inside for them. The hand head people share the mystic of the palm. The old have seen it before. They remember people who used to wear their hair in thick white dreadlocks, flung behind their heads, in a finger like spread. The hair would bounce as if it was a hand playing musical instruments. Fingers, fingers everywhere, are dripping down their back and holding their clothes together.

The hand-head people had words that last through eternity, just like Jeasus, because their infinite palm faces contained their infinite mouths. She would be recorded, like their bible people had been, and be only expected to say good or wise things. The ancient scribes had added both bad and good in their bible, as well as maps clothed in stories, and chemical concoctions dressed with names. It was because children may become what they remembered, that they had hid criminal descriptions in moral stories. She was good, even back then, centuries before, when she was bad.

The hand-head people used to travel in cart caravans of people who travelled the UK, to see the world through the eye of a needle. The needle was part of a map illusion, of when England and Ireland were thought to resemble part of a European spinning wheel, and the miniature capital cities of the thirteen meridian line were the world that fitted through the eye of the needle. The number 13 was like a hemming stitch, they said, as they wore out the thread, tread, on their travels.

Most of the later travellers started at Brighton, and wriggled their way, like another piece of cotton, to London.

The foot on the sewing machine is Italy, as its tide runs in and out, and the sound echoed in a rythmatic beat at the festivals.

The countries were a treasure hunt to find the connections. The facts and figures slip in and out, inter-weaved by thin threads of easy coincidence, and simple minded illusions. They are connected with numerology, and playful mathematics..

The aurora was the tip of the imaginary needle, as it sewed itself counties and countries. It was carrying the red silk thread of the dress of the sunrise and sunset through time. That is what some of the people think they remember, before the fairytales.

In the fairytales the princess sits in her high tower – the palm one of infinite proportions that makes it a pyramid – and pricks her finger with the needle, and there is a drop of blood, which is the aurora. She makes a wish, for a baby. She sheds tears, which land at her feet. The tear drops turn into rough pearls, which become half buried pyramids, sunk into the too dry sand, still in tear shape, as they bounce off her foot. It is an ironic tale when it is transferred to Egypt. The baby that is born is Ireland.

Rapunzel, rapunzel, let down your hair, so the eye may climb without a stare. England is Rapunzel, with foggy, smoky air, which hides anything that travels above it. The eye clouds, which may or may not be space ships, appear and no one notices, while everyone is using coal, and smoke is in the way. They are unmentioned and forgotten, and similar to Shannon's extra eyes. The cloud eye is the eye of the invisible needle of the aurora.

*

But the populace were bored, and overloaded with information, as Shannon is. They may, in search of hysterical excitement, stretch her head out as their new map of the sky. They could pull her skin tight using her hair, and measure distances and stray strands with their cheap school equipment. Her forehead spot will be their north pole, and her fake eyes their spaceships. They will use pea shooters on her, to bring them down, and look at the sky to see if they are gone after hitting her forehead. They will expect to find ear shaped countryside where they have calculated them to be, using her head. They thought they knew her spells and curses, from the old and long gone. She was a seer, a 'Sih' with those moles on her arm, and a sneer, with that raised nostril. Her eyes were being tinted as she was thrown through the clouds. She is a baby reincarnated from their disgusting habits, catching the dirty sky as she teleports. They will search her head with a magnifying glass, looking for other signs of spaceships and of a god, and call nit eggs grains of sand.

They may also think that her bleeding scratches are proof that she, the new born baby, has arrived from Egypt, through the aurora. They might say she had been knocking away the black Egyptian ladybird that is their mosquito, as she was transported. It is shaped like a black mole in a permanent disguise as it hunts for blood and they will see her face and presume that the mole there is the same mosquito, frozen by the air as she flew through time and space. They will remember long dead tales about the same round black beetle.

173

They will think that if it is placed in the middle of their foreheads to suck blood, it will make their eyes lighter, as they thought it had done to her. Some would slice the head from the body of the insect once it had attached itself to the skin, leaving its legs and numbing bite embedded. It would paralyse muscles, like botox did, to give them their Egyptian eyes, they thought. They had mistaken themselves for the insect they had just be-headed. They will buy the bugs off stinking traders, and tempt it to land on their own temple, with a smear of their own blood, and a pray to the heavens, for the same look.

*

They were a typhoid and malarian ridden crowd, eager to establish their right to cold customs, so she would have to take care, when she is born, not to mistake them for friends either.

*

Chapter 10

The Horis sometimes drop the 'H' from their name. Oris is a name they like. Or his, Or hers, they say to each other and others with a knowing glance. On one hand, they could be, on the other, maybe not. Either, or, will do. They are now known as Ors and Whores to themselves. Ori kills. Ori culls. Oracle. That is them. They know what is going to occur, because they have planned it.

Those that watch X rated films have named themselves horrors; the after eleven o'clock scary and frightening film. They do not need the 'H' at the beginning of their name, because it is on television for them already.

The time and name are an obvious reference to themselves, they think. It is the eleventh Hour so it implies the eleventh month. They count the seconds of film, to fourteen, for the first scream or scare. The films are like themselves they say. They start to call their children 'little horrors.' The TV told them to do it.

The films are slash and dash. Mostly, and nearly always, there is a blonde, blue eyed beauty being chased through a wood by something, or someone, with a knife. She wears a bikini. The Horrors cannot see any evil and are memorised by the flashing pictures. They joke about the caesarean section, and pregnant mothers are told that 'they are not out of the woods yet,' by spiteful Horis horror nurses, who smile inanely.

Shannon knows it is her being chased. She was blue eyed and blond, but has turned darker because of her stigmata. The horror films are talking about her minuscule slice and dice skin complaint, and it is she that isn't out of the woody womb yet.

The horror films are played loudly, so the screams of the actor victims waken other households, and confuse the police, who are beginning to jump at every alarm.

The wind carries the sound, so it begins to sound like a hysterical audience, or a hurricane landing. It upsets people, but the freedom of others is still a belief, so nothing can be done.

The electrical power cuts, though, coincidently, start to happen more frequently after ten thirty pm, and the world is plunged into silence again.

*

When Shannon's mother starts to get labour pains, it is a shock to them both. Her mother is watching a film, a horror film, and eating salt and vinegar crisps when the first contraction squeezes Shannon. The electricity turns itself off at the same time, and her mother is genuinely scared.

She is alone and static as she shivers at the unknown.

*

In their fantasy of ownership, by being able to transform their blue eyed babies into brown eyed babies, through drugs and drink, gives the mothers control over naïve and illegal foreigners too. They are Eternal Mother, teacher and next of kin. The black cult also claims to be the Eternal Mother because the womb is dark. Take care, and goodbye Shannon, whispers the voice, either or both of the thick, sick mothers are yours. They may smother you or cover you, depending on their mood and how many drugs they think they have taken.

The voice is fading, and the hands of the womb are twisting her around, ready to be born.

The drugs are the grass, that gets them high, and the words are meant to insult. The grass gets thrown high, as the machine furrows, or as

177

the farmer throws the weed clot up in the air, to get rid of the mud stuck underneath. It will get you high, say the drug dealers. The clods look like hair. The straight hair is the straw coloured tufts of grass, which sits on one side. The roots of the grass are frizzy black cupid hair that sits on the other side. The farmer, with his garden fork, looks as if he is tossing a head in the air. It gets you high. They are playing at being farmers, and they are farming the people, with connective lies.

The farmers' earth turns black, under and enclosed, within the decaying straw, with just the heat of the sun to help the rot. That is what the drug dealers are also selling. They are selling Black, hashish, as if they are selling Asian slaves. They are selling cocaine, choked cane, as if it were white slaves. Every action and name is layered in duplicity, in their world of retarding words. They want to be the farmers they are watching.

The envied farmers are burning the switches, – the roots of the weeds- but no, not really. They are left in a heap until they have dried out, then they are moved, leaving a circle of blackened earth beneath them. It is another burning bush, without real flames. Hail Jaesus, who is a miracle or mirage, for those that do not know how the chemicals are catalysed. Their habits are repeated and slurred, by the cults, to make it sound as if the farmers are medieval and slow in their habits. They are burning witches, they convey with their eyes. They will isolate the innocent, and then take their place. Criminals don't like those that have friends.

When there is an earthquake or hurricane, it is important to remove the bodies and vegetation as quick as possible otherwise the gases of the decomposing can start a fire. The news reports call the explosions that are caused by them terrorist attacks, but it is the revenge of the dead, not the living that is evident. The government has to blame terrorists because it shows a lack of control, on all levels, if the bodies have been left to rot. It shows an unworthy government, and land won't be sold if this is the case. The decomposing give one last gassy fart that reacts with other gases and liquids.

Shannon isn't sure, but thinks alcohol is one of the substances made by the body that will cause the chemical fire.

Babycham, and baby bang.

She is marred and mangy, without her mother being dead, and she is re awoken, in the womb still. Lucky her, that she isn't laying in a bubbling corpse, that would have left her the same kind of skin.

*

Hash is to relax the muscles of the vagina, they say, ready for birthing, like curry being once sold as an abortion method, because it causes a gassy intestine. It makes the anus expel wind, and the vagina will copy, they were told. Hash is smoked, and held in a deep breath, before being expelled with an exaggerated breath. The deep breathe that is held, is the ratio equivalent to the nine months in the womb. The birth is the exhaled smoky breathe, and the hashish is the baby after birth. The head is being substituted for a womb, the cigarette for a penis.

*

The mother should take care, as they may start to try and feed the vagina, or try to teach it to speak. The world is disappearing into shit. Shannon knew, by her own body's disguises.

*

The hash bought is a veiled threat, a seesaw of intent; a completion of the symmetry that they have created; symmetry and cemetery. The symmetry rocks on the black hole of the belly, which is seen as a world, by some, and the face and womb are the two ends that rock.

The baby has already been cremated, they say, and replaced by one of their own, as they blow out smoke.

The buyer is unknowingly agreeing to a blacker world.

Hash is sold in a flattened ball shape, a little bigger than a ten pence piece. It is a big pill that the drug users pay for, as they pay the big bills for the drug dealers. They play with words, and then just pay, out of the habit of paying.

People like her mother pay for the status that being a drug user gives. They are seen as helpless and not responsible for their actions. They have been duped. They like being children, as they heard they were, as they sat in the womb listening to the world discuss the map of the world. They are an 'it', a thing already of the land, of the earth. They are the United Kingdom too, in their embryo form.

They will be the same when they grow as big as the land they are in allows them to. They are big babies, not knowing whether they were to be buried before they had lived. They were born with accusing eyes and a defensive nature. The drugs are rarely authentic or real, but they still pay.

The generation before were all nature and zoo. They were hamster features and bushy eyed. Their beards were tusks, and bums stuck out in four legged impersonation of the animal world. They were all that was in front of their parents eyes. They were beasts and flowers that walked in human form. They searched the skies for signs of cloud change, and sniffed the air for new comers. They ate the knotted roots of weeds, and chewed on dandelion leaves as they set fire to fallen buildings, to halt the dead's gasses spreading. They knew how many dead there was by how bright the fire burnt, and there in the sky, for them, the aurora was the torch of the dead. Gas meets gas as fallen cities group under the ice, pushed there by volcanic tides and horrendous winds. The ice compacts and freezes

180

as it heats, and the dead are thermos flasked. They are geysered out particles in hot water, to be pushed into the sky, leaving the red road of skyline to show the world that they once existed. The aurora demanded to be noticed for its human sacrifices, that were victims of the weather.

When a dead baby was born the mother was sometimes accused of conspiring with the winds of the aurora, by the superstitious. She begets what she coveted. She stared at the aurora, and a woman of the church stared at the statue.

The hurricanes move scythe like over the world, before being dragged back to the aurora, leaving the dead to gas the ice again, teach the Horis.

*

The story of the day is about immigrants again.

The illegal immigrants are selling Horis food on the streets, without a license. They are inspired by the kebab shop and the samosas are lined up, like dinosaur scales, on newspapers, outside them. They have made the samosas themselves, after raiding bins and gardens. They are made of spiced vegetable or meat and is served hot or cold, states the news report. It is hot even when it is cold, and the pastry is made using very thin pastry, and it is fried. The pastry is named 'filo', 'Fly low.' or 'Feel low', by others, who imagine the street samosas are like diarrhoea filled nappies.

The outside of it, that used to be a gooey red, had changed colour since it was first popular. It used to be served at parties held in honour of the dead and in honour of the aurora, to keep the blood and hands warm. The colour of it had been too similar though, to rough and blistered work hands, as if the palm had been peeled and used to sandwich the innards.

181

But now, in this segment of ill timing, there was a re living of ancient history to change history. The illegal immigrants wanted to take the natural residents place in the re telling of events. They wanted control of the food, as they heard the enemy should have, and, like the Horis and their symbolism, they strove to convince people that they had always had control of it, since the beginning. They had always been here, they implied, but unnoticed. The immigrants laid the samosas on the newspapers, and watched as flies buzzed around them. They waited for health inspectors, who no longer existed, to make an appearance. The hurricane wind came and went, and in between was the soaring heat, and themselves. They enjoyed flashing the past out of old grey charity shop overcoats and shocking the law abiding.

The weather isn't mentioned, and the flooding inland ignored by the same newspapers.

The cult of the Horis was dis-banded a long time ago, and to see the parody of the unpopular people line the streets make the few who remember the violent cult uncomfortable. They have echoed the fashion of the cult in their clothes, hairstyles and jewellery too. It is a pre Raphaelite gathering, in a blackened print, out of time and context.

White to black to white again, as they slip into corners and side streets.

It may be the setting of the pattern of how her life may be, slipping into black clothes and streets, and out again.

She will need, with her uneven nose, their out-of-date decorations. She will need a nose clip to straighten the nostrils. She will hunt out a Creole earring from the past, a real one; that is, a nose ring, with weights on it, to pull one side of her face down to normal proportions. She will borrow a black blanket, an abayas, to hide her tainted brow, and a pale, flesh coloured bindi to hide her whitened mole. She will feint and flash into darkness, as she is doing now, flashing her ugliness to the world.

*

The room where her mother was was overcrowded with things. As there was no light, she stumbled and slipped on discarded clothes and empty mugs as she searched for her mobile phone. She was slovenly, and the phone had fallen under a pile of loose jumpers. As she reached for it, her and Shannon suffers another sharp pain.

Shannon will be Alice again, falling down the hole. She will have a double head band, when she squeezes through the vagina, as her head will stay for a second or two within the clown's wig of pubic hair that sits there.

It is fitting for her clown appearance.

In the light of day there will be another streak, an imprint, from the white mole to the end of her brow, which impersonates an age line and part of the palm print. It will look like a shooting star and the clowns painted-on brow, too high in the forehead. She will forever be half surprised. The small penny shaped mark that lies on each cheek are obvious in the day light too. They are small Pierrot cheeks, exaggerated by the clown into larger reddened circles. Her mouth has its own pouch and will be clown like as she ages, and her thin curly hair will be white and bouncy, with its tiny bald spot. She will have to join the circus, and be ironic, with her one fake raised eyebrow, and raised lip, but, with a sense of self preservation, she knows that she will not go to them, because she won't be accepted by them, because she is a clown. She knows that just because the elephant cartoon is funny, it doesn't mean a real elephant is wanted.

And there they are again, in the background, the voyeurs of other peoples lives. They have beauty counter whitened faces and over

183

rouged round cheek bones. The hair is permed and dyed to unnatural colours. The lips are reddened. Their shoes are heeled, and they break one, in public places, to echo mismatched bodies. They match her looks at every thought. They are a mass of clones, being the few natural clowns. Shannon feels overwhelmed with pity for them, as she realises. Some swallow the few whole, but there are people who don't want to see the mirror in their friend or enemy. They want to be different and the least envied, so they won't be copied, but they all think the same. It is then their fashion instead of their disguise.

She will be uglier than she thought she would be when she is born but she has designed herself to please the religious and curious. In this hysterical time, she will please all of the people all of the time, as they search for answers, and therefore live longer.

She knows all and everything, about the old stories that they were told. She knows that the Jack-in-the-box is someone like her, a clown caught within their moles, which makes invisible lines to form a cube. She knows the meaning of the playing cards and of the joker. She knows the tarot cards and the dice as if she had been told for years. All men and women are the king and queen cards. The women are doubled lunged as the womb breathes slowly, flooding itself with oxygenated blood. They are the lungs of the invisible twin and the pubes are the hair. The men are thought to have two brains, with their testes sac as the other one, which doubles as a nose. The numbered cards are aliments, sins, and the mixtures of genes. The card games are all genetic inheritance and resulting dominant features.

The genitals are a decoy for the baby human's face. They are placed where the human can see them, by looking down. The person that feeds the wrong end, the imbecile, can then be observed and dealt with, with swinging arms and poisoned shit, as the baby body pretends regurgitation, in imitation of bird-like behaviour, and

184

defecates and urinates instead. It would be swallowed up by the idiot, along with what fell back out. It was survival of the most sensible.

When it is a society that tries to feed the wrong end, the more basic their world is, and the more likely food would be placed in front of a penis to be sniffed, instead of held to the nose. The reversal starts as they bloat their bowels until their mouths start to shit by vomiting. They turn the body around as if it has a multi use. They are anal sex, and melon genital soaped, and they can't walk away because their feet are shoulders. They have paper towels for their mouths, while their anuses drink water from bidets. It is happening around her mother.

They seem to have mis-watched their surroundings again, and mistaken USB slots for human orifices, and human orifices for Office. They have invented sluts, and have lost their IQ, and taste.

Shannon's mother sits with her legs wide open, to give her womb lungs air. She believes it is an entity by itself. She is a two totem pole person, and her husband is another two. Together they are a four legged beast, with the beast head in their hand.

Two and two makes one, the baby, and she throws an Ace on top of the king and queen. Ace high, the baby is nigh; Ace low, time to go: the baby is ready to be born.

Shannon is the Joker and her other mini face is the jokers stick.

*

And Christ is dice, and dice are racks of mouldy meat. Seven is the spine, with its coccyx end. Christ on the cross, bent up backwards to make the dice.

*

Remember it all, she tells herself, but remember to tell them first that they have to wait to see your miracles, so you live a little longer. Tell them about your Holy Ghost smile, which will appear on your face,

185

in February, on the fourteenth. Tell them it will appear from the edge of your lip towards your ear; lines of scratches which will make a mouth shape. It is your Mona Lisa smile, which cannot be captured on film. They will glove your hands in mittens, and stand back with trepidation of what they see, when you do not scratch. Miracles do not happen in their mostly germ free world. They will think it is a mirage caused by hot skin and a refraction of light, but then they will look at your ghost eyes, and know.

The shadow lips are your Valentines and Romeo's too.

Valentine sneaks in from behind pale curtains. The gathered curtains are facial muscles, muscles made easier on the eyes by everyday disguise. Sometimes, in the story, the curtains are red, or flowered. Flowers, she thinks, are acne.

Don't forget to tell them, Shannon, as soon as you are born. Show them your melanin head to hold their attention, and tell them to wait for your extra smile.

*

The hospital has been rung, just like it is supposed to be rung, according to the scenarios of giving birth.

There is no one to answer it. They are not used to the drama bad weather brings, as it hardly ever happens as far inland as they are, and are understaffed. The emergency generator is supporting the hospital, and trolleys of people are being rushed here and there. Other hospital people have not appeared at work. They have been unable to travel through impassable roads.

Some of the volunteer emergency workers are cleaning floors, unblocking drains and securing objects that would otherwise fly away in the high winds. Bikes fly, and cars swivel. Plant pots and ladders are lifted into the air with ease. Small, loose stones break windows, and garden sheds slide. They are busy being good and the

186

phones ring as if they are tinny church bells, echoing into empty offices.

Her mother's emotions fly high too, as she catches and latches on to the excitement of distress. She becomes the star of the silent film, calling in the darkness, with no subtitles to help the audience. Her film is scratched and aged too, by flying brambles and twigs.

The yellow street lights are still working, surrounded by houses in darkness, giving her mother the sepia light she needs to complete the damsel look.

Suddenly, and inexplicably, though, the wind calms and the lights flicker on again. Her mother is grabbing at her skirt, near her vagina with both hands, and her mouth is rounded. Her friend is videoing it all with her mobile phone.

Her father catches hold of her arm, with urgency, and tries to rush her to his big heavy van, to drive her to the hospital.

They race against another power cut, to reach the van before the lights go out again. They are hunched, and casting shadows in all directions, as the lights in neighbouring houses brighten. A gust of wind makes her mother give a quick shout before the van door is shut. They are safe inside, and driving. Shannon jogs and sleeps through the obstacles on the road. She is nearly born in to the crushing but beautiful world. She is ready to smile benignly and to tell them, without words, what she is before she is sacked or sold.

She is hoping that she is wrong, about it all though. She doesn't want the complication of criminals or cranial deformities to spoil her birth. She was probably hearing muscle contraction and pumping blood, she thinks, or it is muffled knowledge through layers of skin and blood. There have been experiments about it all. The qualities of sound through different mediums; like water waves through water the air waves echo through milk, blood and blisters. It leaves a

187

different accent, echo, as it passes through each density. It reverberates, and changes love in to loathe. It is a spell binder, all by itself; a causer of wars and passions. Soon, she will see and hear whether it is true or not. Whether she is a creature or a human born of the Fair Eire land, and its Kingdom.

The van halts outside the hospital, which is quiet, and too busy to be so quiet. There are no moans or groans from the patients, with their differing ailments, just shocked faces. The cuts are wrapped in paper or tea towels, and twisted limbs in gentleness. They are lined in seats, waiting for the number of their ticket to be called. The seats are all full, and some of the people are leaning on walls, and washing themselves in hospital bathrooms, turning the sinks red with blood. The toilets themselves are full of vomiting food poisoned victims.

Shannon can hear help bubbling through on mobile phones and CB radios. Some of the emergency farm workers have casualties in the toilets, and they are heading towards the hospital anyway. An off duty doctor is gently being persuaded to return to work, and he is telling them of others that can spare a few hours. She will born and meet these kind people. They will give her charitable looks, and clean her with sterilised cloths.

Her mother is speaking on a mobile too, with deep exaggerated breathes in between each set of words, and in a low tone. She was in the toilets, struggling with the other women for toilet space. As she is pregnant she is given priority and whispers behind the closed toilet door.

Shannon sleeps, and moves.

She is Alice with the chalice. The chalice sits on her foot, and she sits in the chalice, the womb. The womb is also a cup, and a two handed porringer. The toilet bowl is an echo of the chalice womb, and she wonders if she will slip from one to the other, from red to white, because she is blue. The chalice sits under her foot skin, shaped out of blue veins, and rests on the front of her toes, reaching to her ankle, across her foot. The chalice is the result of over exertion.

If she was born in another era it would be said that she had walked enough already, before she was born, and would be given a coach to travel in.

It is the Chalice that the Knights look for, but can never find, because they are always looking to the sky for it, as if they were in England looking for the aurora, and its grail shape, on the wrong day.

They never look down in time to see it on their feet, as a warning to rest. By the time the veins bulge on their faces, their faces look as if they were entwined in tree branches, and they are dead from exhaustion. It is birth, as she struggles to untangle herself from the tree branch arteries of the womb. She is Knight and Lady, hanging, with her foot nearly exposed to the polluted sterilised air of the bathroom.

There is another rudimentary face made of three burrs, which have just appeared on her foot. They are shaped as two round red eyes, and a cartoon 'D' mouth. The face sits above her big toe, seemingly in front of the bunched blue veins. It looks like a feint, sepia black and white photo of a tourist in front of Brighton Palace.

While Shannon is unconscious, her foot reaches towards the soft tissue of the cervix. It is a frightened instinct, to test the hostility of the world.

The blue veins stand out with the effort, and the chalice can be seen clearer.

This is calculated. Shannon is like a cunning animal dealing with a very stupid one. Her mother will reach for Shannon's foot, which is disguised as a drinking glass, fooled into thinking it is her dropped

189

alcohol, and pull her out of herself. Shannon will be pulled with greed and will be freed.

The chalice foot is full of blood, and in the room that she will be born in will be full of Cult and Chrystians, so it is brave of her, she thinks, to attempt this trick. Her last-minute bowling bowl marks on her foot are an attempt to disguise it as one of themselves. They do not attack themselves unless they are sure they can do it without being caught. It will appear as if she is a drinker or a church goer, by looking at her foot. She will also be mosque visitor and aurora worshipper, if they glimpse in its direction. She will please all of the people, for a little of the time that she needs for the next step of survival.

They will perhaps, try to pull her out either way in their conversion of her mind, if they see what she imagines is there. They will take turns pulling at her limbs, like bell ringers. One will pull at her foot, and will be moved by their nemesis, who will pull at her other one, when it emerges. They will stop when they get to her head, and realise that they have already split her, and put her back together. She is the judgement of King Solomon, reincarnated to haunt the agreeing but wrong mother who is giving birth to her.

But she will be safe until then, and afterwards they will have to take care of her, less their morals show. They have to hide their views from each other because they don't trust each other to agree with them. No one knows whether they stand next to one that feels the same as themselves. Their world runs on hints and tips, but never words that can implicate crime. It is the fear of being caught that halts the hand that would pull and twist her foot off. The fear of standing alone in their bloody morals too, after being told all their life that everyone was the same when no one was looking, that makes them pause. If they are good people, they will be replaced for their reputation, and because they help and do not hinder.

Shannon is echoing the United Kingdom again as she struggles to turn around. She is baby Ireland, sitting next to the pelvic bone that is England. Scotland's Hadrian's Wall is the division and emphasis of the pelvic bone shape. Stonehenge is the base of the spine. The military are long ago bored artists and Shannon's foot is standing on the wall, while her head peers at Cornwall. To be born her head has to be by Scotland.

*

They are in a room at the hospital.

The nurse, who is long and blonde, is Ors, and a sometimes Chrystian. She takes drugs and visits festivals, picking up dropped money and forgotten bags. She managed to obtain the job by sending in a CV that wasn't hers, with a name that wasn't hers. The only thing she shared with the woman who she claimed to be was her face, which was pretty and innocent looking.

The doctor, who believed her as long as she believed him, was an illegal who took pronunciation lessons after spotting his double entering a hospital in a different county. He is contrarily and unbelievably devoutly religious. His duplicity doesn't bother him. There is also a midwife, who is the only one who is qualified. She edges the outskirts of all the birthing rooms, elbowing her way in when she sees the mother having difficulties. She is a mimer, and never talks, when she doesn't have to, to other people.

There are two women who have appeared, who have looked through into the room, as if they are enquiring family or friends. They are neither. It is usual for strangers to behave as they are intimate, as if they are brothers or aunts, sisters and cousins. In high emotion they are easily confused for the real blood relatives, and they take advantage of this, so all visitors are smiled at politely before being shut out.

*

If her foot helps her survive, she will pamper it. She will cover her foot with an ankle bracelet that has chain mail and a toe ring. The chain mail will be made of gold, diamonds and sapphires, and the toe ring will be platinum. The jewellery will suit it's wealthy Russian background, and it's mythical church connections. The beads will disguise her crucifixion mole.

When she is born the face on the foot will be hardly seen, but the audience is a huddle of dumbed, attentive, animals that have been startled into their animal-like alter ego by bad weather and passing corpses. The doctor will squint his eyes, and the actress nurse will halt in mid step, without knowing why. It is the hint her foot gives, that it is one of a triplet, to say Shannon is not alone, that more are following, that makes them pause. They do not attack groups.

The people in the room are also thinking of the chances of getting home alive. They haven't been trained to deal with the hurricane situation, on the scale of death and devastation. They have been trained to tame windy breezes, and two inch flooding. They cannot comprehend how these things happen when they have never happened before, and stand stupid amongst the chaos.

Shannon wants someone definite to be near, someone who knows what to do. She cannot stand the feeling that no one is in control.

The emergency farm workers are on their mobiles and are cleaning the corridor, while a priest nearby says a last prayer for the dead, before they are wheeled away. They will help her, when they realises. The womb relaxes, and bitty blood clots wet the sheets underneath.

192

Her chalice foot is turning around.

It is a celebration already, she thinks, that she has made it this far. She will get married, and her husband will celebrate her cunning foot by drinking wine out of her bridal slipper shoe. It is a hazy scene that she has imagined. Mouth, blood, and foot are entwined. Shannon shrinks. The groom drinks the foot, as the blood flows down the bottle shaped leg. Her grail foot is seen as an invite, a literal drinking glass, and they are drinking from it. Her foot is another hand, balancing a glass for them to sample her blood. Her bowels are their partner, conspiring towards her death; their other half that they are marrying, not her. She will be passed on, when she has passed away. She is picture card, betrayed by her Siamese twin into a vamperic existence. She will not get married, then, but will be forever living-in-sin, cos and tan instead. They will make angles of her. She will be the bends of slavery. Sharp cornered spine and elbows, as she does others' housework. She will listen instead, while she works, to the women who still break and bend their stiletto shoe forward, to make a loose bottle shape, before attacking with it, in delayed reaction, in memory of their imagined ancestors. There is a gaping open mouth space in the scrunched shoe where the distorted label or her grail cup veins would fit. They hold the broken shoe by the heel, from behind, as if offering a glass to drink from, when they are thinking of stabbing someone with it.

The crucifixion beauty spot that balances above her chalice foot hints of poison and suicide pills, to stop the blood drinkers, if they are still there lingering like dogs by her toes, from moving closer. The blistered heels of the foot are the cork of the wine bottle and spill out water, as if to entreat the enemy to drink that instead.

And Jeasus turned wine into water and showed beast how to be human

There is blood about Shannon and it is giving her nightmares.

*

The ballet shoes that hang off the closet hook become feet and the ribbons, the bones. They are tibia and fibula, and the ballet dancers have legs that go all the way up to their arse, and the closet hook is the slit of the vagina. The closet is the larder, and Shannon feels sick in her throat.

She is not a cat any more; she is a pole cat, even though she has not grown. She is stretched out, long and lithe, ferret like. Ballet slipper shaped as the placenta leaves.

The cults will eat each other into an empty extinction. There will be no monument, no art nor literature to show they have ever been. She is ferret, which is Faerie. Ferret baby is a name passed around. The cults spit it at each other and see who it sticks to in each era, as the embryos grow hairier in response to the icy winds. It is the turn of women to be dehumanised as the words warp and they are named the ferret sects, pronounced the 'fairer sex'. They were told to cling to trouser legs and that, when they grew up, they will hang on to men's necks, in an impersonation of expensive fur, like they used to do in the past. The women were told they were too hairy, and their babies were stoats in bleached boats when they are giving birth, by media advertising and bitchy street gossip.

The cults supposedly threw these words at each other through the news medias too, but they didn't. It is what the newspaper reporters heard as they walk through silent hospitals that started the hatred. They are, like Shannon, cocooned, but by their beliefs, and misheard silent gossip that wasn't meant for their ears. The silent chatters were talking of the hurricane that had hovered above, to the left of the UK. They were using their bodies as the land in their explanation, and

194

talked about zooming in, not women. The bleach boats had overturned, they told each other, as had the ferry. The North Sea wind powered turbines had sunk, causing major power loss in Scotland too. It had happened before, in the past.

This head line is not in the papers while sexual equality stays front page news.

*

The blood on the bed is a Rorschach inkblot test for the people in the birthing room. They have been staring at it blankly, as if they cannot think of a story to tell an enquiring psychologist, of why they are staring blankly at spreading blood. They do not really know why themselves. Their varying strong beliefs, which once spurred them into some kind of excitement, had dwindled into a mild twinge of undirected longing.

The nurse, who once saw the opportunity for baby swapping and making additional money, realised almost at once that the CCTV camera wouldn't allow for these extra activities, and had resigned herself to looking pretty in the hope that a doctor would fall for her charms. The doctors, knowing she wasn't quite what she seemed, had relegated her to the foreign doctors, who were usually married to the same foreign wives. She would not be able to swap places easily.

She does not drink baby blood, despite, or perhaps because of her Ors upbringing, and is unaware of the suspicions of the doctors. She lives her life in a twilight world of the Horis, and the more calming atmosphere of the hospital. The nurse is aware of e.coli and salmonella, of staphylococcus aureus and avian flu. A baby, she thinks, is more like chicken, and is un healthy until proven otherwise. Babies, with their quick growth, would not heal with their forming blood, but cause cancers, as the isolated cells congealed to make bone, hair and teeth. They will not keep her young, as botox does,

195

either. She is not insane, like her ancestors. The blood gently reminds her to book another appointment with her beautician.

The immigrant doctor looks for the hair and skin that will follow the blood. He has been taught to eat the animals that do not have veins and toes, arteries and nails. He eats the hoofed and makes cups from the horn. He will eat chicken, and swan, but not the crow, which is as forbidden as the cow used to be. These people also do not eat anything black. The colour is untouchable in the world of edible consumerism. Black animals and food are safe from their appetites. Shannon is blue and red. The blue veins look like underlying black. She is inedible, despite her pig like birthplace.

The midwife swiftly massages the womb, causing Shannon to withdraw her attempts of being born.

She hides the movements of her hand under the sheet that covers the rest of Shannon's mother, so the others in the room do not imitate her.

Shannon's mother has everything covered, except her vagina. She is a bride again, for the illegal immigrant doctor. Her pelvic bones mimic the shape of an opened skull. Her vagina is a nose about to form, and a mouth opened wide in singing. The other mouth is the anus and it expels wind in an attempt at vocals. Her white covered legs are hunched arms. Some used to think that it is not a simile, but a truth. They thought the body was two, by itself. The stomach talks in rumbles and growls as if it was a dog. When they met their partner, their partner took their stomachs place. They kept their partner in the dark, clothed in black and vagina mouth hidden. They are their shame, and their silent partner; brainless, but who knew all their secrets. The block colour cult claims to be this other half too, as they cover everything but their noses.

The doctor could, if her mother dies, take a new bride, with her birth certificate and her name. The death will not be registered, but the corpse shoved in to the hall, with the rest. The rumour of child brides hints at 'chilled brides' who are the dead women, legs still spread and dressed in a white sheet, who are suddenly re married to a different man, and have re appeared as a different colour. So chilled, their skin has turned frost bite black.

The new woman who walks away with her life is called a sulky studying child, no matter how old. They are the lower half of the dead woman, who was never seen before. They are called students because of the way the legs look like arms, and the way the pubic hair resembles a bent head, as if it was bent in study. They are child, because their names are born from the chilled. The shadow twin will follow the legally born child through life, like a farmer follows the calf, and claim to be a relative. The criminals gloat about their crimes by calling themselves the student name, and mixing with people who are.

The midwife worries about this, and the crimes committed when she is not there. One wrong movement could cause severe damage, and she doesn't want to be responsible for their amateur attempts at midwifery, or to be blamed after she has left. The sheet is held high, and she is in and out of the room before any one can stop her, taking her silence with her.

She has no beliefs; she thinks that she is neither Chrystian nor cult. She was taught, from when she was a child that she would be a midwife, and she does not question. She was given a husband, and told she would have children. She was told which names to give them, and what profession the children would have. This would stop her worrying about them, and prolong her life; she will look younger than most for a very long time. She is content, and has wooden

197

shutters that protect her home from the hurricanes. There are rain barrels for water, and a hidden solar panel for electricity. The solar panel is a new addition, one that her family took time in considering in its implementation. The home, her home, was given to her along with her job and family, and it will be given to the next mid wife after she has died, so she has to consider her feelings when making important decisions. If her husband dies, she will phone the hospital. Another twin husband will then move in, so the status quo is not upset. She does not know what an 'insect' person is. The people she interacts with are trained professionals and her way of life is a sensible one.

*

Shannon's shadow eyes, her holy ghost, take another guise as her mother scans the room warily; the muscles contract, and the Scarborough aquarium, which is the opera house of Australia, morphs out of the reddened skin of her shadow eyes. It is an artist's impression of how the opera house would look. Red, as it is imagined hot. The blue veins above her real eyes, but below her fake one, ripple with strain to give the appearance of a calm ocean sea that the aquarium sits in.

Stonehenge appears on the back of her shoulder, as a ring of spots.

It will come and go, like the other marks. Her arm is Devon, when England is England, but is a pointy continent when her body is the world.

Stonehenge is the cog of clocks hands. Devon, Cornwall and Wales are the arm and hand. It was always five past twelve or one o'clock. Most call it the thirteenth hour. There are statues of Jaesus with one arm tied up, and the other dangling. Her west County arm is the one tied up. The other dangling arm is the southern continents.

When Africa and India are the clock hands, then Stonehenge would be in Moscow. Moscow sits on the shoulder of Finland, which is the arm of Europe. Her mind fits the world together like a puzzle. When she is born, she will fit one on top of the other, and know the world's secrets, of centuries before. She is big and small again, with Alice in Wonderland growth and shrinkage.

She will to announce at them, in a dramatic pose, when she is born, 'I am your whole year, and your whole world, and here I am whole.'

They will spit out apologies, and turn their backs as she dresses herself. They will find her a golden pillow made of honey, and she will sleep and eat, in comfort and peace, at last. She dreams in her sleep, as her mother is given drugs to help her be born.

The Roof tops of Russia are the cogs and wheels that make the time, and the balancing wheel is Stonehenge. Moscow is the eye of the head, which is bent over the work table, as the Scandinavian hand picks them both up, and makes them a watch or clock. Italy is the leg seen under the table.

The spell of the Atlas tightens over Shannon. She is spellbound and hungry to see it.

She will travel over time, through time, as the hours go forward and backwards. She will ski over the white sleeves of the watch maker, down his neck, and into the air of Russia. She will sit on the table, and then slide down the leg of Italy, before falling on to the magnified mirror of Africa.

She will change herself to show her travels. Her hair will be worn extra long, parted in the middle, with the hair gathered in rubber bands, to hang on the breasts. They will be worn in very low bunches, to look like egg timers, just how they used to be worn. She will wear circular head decorations above her ear. One will be a small Stonehenge circle, and the other a larger Moscow with its golden tops. They will be micro, micha, mocha fashion, revived for the nineteen hundreds.

The hair is suited to her now unfashionable lopsided head.

She will slip through, to the other half of history, and the other half of the world, and let people know what she is thinking as she walks.

Then she will change and wear her hair piled on top of her head, and wear globular, circle earrings, instead. They will show time in miniature, but will be seen as America and Africa too. The hair will be inset with tear drop pearl, to show pyramids. Her hair will be powdered white, and her dresses will have bulbous length. She will dance in the mirror, watching far away people ape in imitation, as they act out the Atlas, as they polish the floors. A step to the left, that is Italy, A step backwards for New Zealand, and arms interlinked for the Norwegian countries. They will dance out the globe again, and dance around to imitate the sun, moon, and planets that mark the time.

She will travel forward and backwards through fashion, to suit her body's dictation. To suit it's calendar. The world will dance with her, as she skips continents and twirls around sea shores.

Chapter 11

Her mother's legs had moved as if she had learnt the steps from the television. One was flung to the left and the other to the right. The right leg was slightly bent.

She was teetering on the edge of giving birth, and looks as if she was. She was acting out the event. She was giving a charade to the CCTV audience that she imagined was watching, as her hands clung to the sides of the trolley, and her eyes drifted towards her breast - 'tit'- and then to a ring on her finger. She was 'teet her ring'. Her legs were spread wider as her neck creased forward, and she peered downward at herself. She was giving birth.

The hospital is full of dead people still, bought inland, from the coasts. Her mother was lucky to have been allowed in, and even though she enjoys the negative attention, part of her was full of fear and sanity as she was swept pass the trolleys that were waiting for the morgue. She is stuck in a frozen charade.

It is the reality of the horror films that she feels is in front of her, as if the television did not turn off, but opened like a box to engulf her life.

She had been on a trolley herself, being wheeled through another packed corridor, to the room.

Her legs had spread and now there is blood.

It is the red on the bed.

She said.

The trolley had clashed with the stationary ones, and there had been a quiet panic in the faces of the hospital staff as they had moved past her in either direction. It was a panic directed towards the situation, rather than herself.

Her mother didn't experience the adrenaline rush that normally accompanies horror, but perhaps she needed to see it through a small glass box, like a peeping tom, before the chemicals were triggered.

There is a clip board at the end of each trolley, and the nurse had flicked through them as if they were the credits at the end of the film. Her mother is a film again. She wants to be the centre of everyone's attention, until the credits stop rolling. She wants to divert the hospital staffs attention to the living, herself, else they may echo what they see, and she doesn't want to die, and be pushed back in to the corridor of dead people. She screams.

*

The words warp and wiggle as the hours tick past. Shannon is changing again to suit the death her mother left behind in the corridor.

In another slight change of genetics, hair springs out of her toes and the backs of her fingers. She has been ferreted. It is thick and black, and she sleeps again as a shadow appears under and near her nose. It is a darker patch of skin, in the shape of a snail, to scare away flies and worms. The snot that will run from her nose is its slime trail. The snail has antennas. It is convincing enough to keep the flies out of her nose, so she can breathe. It is a last leap of self survival that causes this change. She is also scared of the nail she has been threatened with, the one her mind thinks is driven through her palm, by the multitude. It understands, it thinks, their low intelligence, and rhymes 'nail', with 'snail'. Shannon can hear the fear through the departing blood. She has refused to stick to the script that has been written for her, and has adapted it. Her blood rhymes. It is the fear of death, that lines the corridor, that mould and rot with maggots that turn into flies, that sends her genes speeding towards her nose. It meant to squeeze it tight, against the smells of sickness and the morgue too, but, lacking fingers, left the good intention imprinted there instead. Its fake snail shadow, will fool and fascinate the eyes of her enemies too, and the spying CCTV cameras, as it appears on its yearly visit.

The hair is a dual purpose of warmth and warning to the flies; that they will sink into her skin, body first, with thick legs left to wave in the breeze as they die. The sparse hair either side of the knuckle also make the fingers look like a line of waxed bikini vaginas, or a pile of leaping spiders, as the hand grabs at nothing. Warmth, warning to the predators, and a sign to those that claim to be short sighted to what she is. No need to touch and pry. There is her sex, on her fingers. Shannon will grow her finger nails long, and scratch women and men that try to touch her. She will leave scars in their botox skin, and loose nails in their mounds of flesh.

*

Her husband will be husbandry, and she will be breeding meat to meet meat, to mate and make more meat, instead of having romance and a bridal gown, if they are allowed to bully her.

She can dream though. She will wait for a prince, who never arrives. She will twiddle her thumbs while she sits and waits for her betrothed to rescue her, and learn to count how long she has waited with her fingers. Twelve months in a year made up from the twelve joints in the fingers of one hand, that doesn't include the thumb. The year of Horis is in her hand, and the male year, on the other hand, has two extra months, includes the thumb as a penis. One hand is months and one hand is hours and weeks.

Spaced on each finger joint are the cycles of the moon, ending in the waxing crescents of the finger nails. Together the hands are twenty six months, split between two years. It is thirteen months a year, in the old world, and the ancient calendar.

204

It is twelve months each year now, with a hidden month sneaked into flight hours and time differences, for accountants.

The numbers speed around Shannon's head.

It is hinted that dogs live to thirteen years. That is in dogs' years.

The calculations are made by using three fingers, because the dog only has three toes, and a claw it tucks into the underneath. Three and one. Thirteen.

They, the Horis public, are obsessed by the two numbers.

The three finger calculation is used with a point of a finger to the ugly people. These are people who haven't had their teeth cosmetically changed, who don't use hairdressers or invent aches and pains for the pharmacy. They are targeted because they don't look the same as the next person. They are, these ugly people, in this new world of invasion and people pyramiding, dog meat and dog. It is now a dog eats dog world, joke the thieves. A dog eats dog country, they laugh, as they find Ireland on the map again, and note that the shape of it is canine like. Targets are called Irish, no matter their nationality. They have saved too much money by being ugly, and the thieves will have it, no matter how small their fortune is.

And her mother laughs too, as she remembers her dad in her sleep.

They are hyenas in their lack of humanity.

*

Shannon's head is suddenly pushed out, and her eyes are level with a flabby white, thick thigh. The light isn't shocking or surprising. It seems normal, and familiar.

She can see, and sense, the tired Chrystians.

They are passing in the corridor, weary and empty. They have worked and puked, and cleaned, and puked. She will be saved. The gap in the door shows them in their kindness. One will turn and see her godliness, and her helplessness. They will take her to a kinder land, and join her on a pilgrimage to find the secrets of time in Europe and Egypt. She will not slide into the London sewers when she lets go of the umbilical cord. They will save their saviour, who knows that their blood is undrinkable.

She will point out her warping melanin head, and her bloods intelligence. She will stop them being slaughtered and eaten, when she tells the world what she knows of the intelligent bacteria, and how it plans the revenge for the murderer, and the cannibal. It will poison and distort their bodies, should they hurt it. It will live in the air, ghost like, waiting for its chance of retribution if its host dies. It knows. It is an entity by itself, but attached to the epidermis. It is the static atomic, life of the skin.

Their enemies, her enemies, will fall back, and become human again, their hysterical appetites forgotten in the fright of self harm through eating her or others. They will remember that her forehead berry mole is poisonous mistletoe, and her strawberry heart mole is an autumn ivy leaf, as their appetites ramble through lost musings.

And she will save them, the Chrystians, by her enemies own insistence that she is inside out and upside down. Her poisonous mistletoe mole was, and is, they say, in the womb too, and is the extra, un-natural teat that she fed off and will feed her babies with. It is the remnants of a sucker, they say. She is a familiar, a cat-child, curled up in the womb, with the extra udder. Her hidden habits have left their mark on her skin, has it has on other Chrystians, they think. That udder though makes her inedible. She is poisonous meat. Foot in mouth, mouth in foot, and mouth in hand. As meningitis ridden as the animals were, she shall say. If her blood or her relative's blood is spilt, it will turn the air alive with its anger. It will be leprosy and the plague for them all again, should they let her Pandora out of the imagined box that is scattered all over her.

But it is her other, extra face, which shows its ghost of a smile that will astound them and stop them all. It is prove of what she is saying. They will be awed anew too, at the sight of the Holy Ghost appearing on earth. Praise be to god, and may Lourds have mercy on their souls.

*

Her mother screams in her sleep again, as if she too senses the Chrystians and is willing one of them to stop and look, to rescue them. Shannon is half way born, and is a dot in the V of her mother's theatrical legs. Her head stings at the corners, as her cigarette burn brow is exposed to the air, and is open, weeping blisters. It looks as if her mother's vagina had grown poisoned fangs and had bit on her.

When she slips out she is quickly placed in a plastic cot, and pads are fixed over her eyebrows with shaking hands. She is too small and a kitten, instead of a cat. They are all fingers and thumbs again, and she is palm. She is made into a white Mickey Mouse by the round pads, and she stares at the nurse and doctor with her small big eyes, and her lip and nostril snarls at them, by itself. She signals them with her eyes, and the stares turn into curiosity.

She is studied with wide, pitying looks that have a hint of smugness.

Ugly child, she reads from their looks. Dripped on and squashed, in the womb, with tainted blood. Money child.

Money's child was full of face, Chews away child was full of haste.

Chews away child is a baby born with a hare lip.

She is half way there, caught in time, squeezed between the days of the week.

The doctor moves closer and bends over, while her mother gulps and snores. He raises his eyebrows, as if he is camouflaging himself to look like her, and moves even closer. His eyes are by her confetti coloured skin, which is her fake eye, which is her rose, and her mini

207

face. 'How,' he whispers at her, with slitty eyes and bad breath, 'did you know?'

The nurse is surprised into curiosity, at his interrogating approach to the new born. It is not usual. Also, he has forgotten to correct his accent, and she is filled with disappointment. Not real, after all. But if he isn't a doctor, she will not be a nurse.

She moves towards Shannon as well.

The doctor's eyes have widened.

'Did you see that?' he asked the nurse, ' Is she telling me that.. that.. means she needs her temperature taking.'

'Is that a face, on her forehead?' The nurse answers.

It is the way the Horis are taught to talk, to avoid detection. Answer a question, with a question. The criminal, when questioned of crimes, will turn into the accuser. The criminal will incriminate the victim of the crime. The hunter will ape the prey.

It is habit that steers the nurse's mouth, while her eyes search for validity in what she thinks may be a hallucination.

Her own words register before the doctors do, and for a moment she is confused. Her opinion is being sought on a medical condition, and if she answers it may show her ignorance. It is there though, she is assured. Two tiny eyes, complete, looking inwards, towards the imagined bridge of a nose. There is a small pig like nose, and an open mouth, as if it was about to speak, and a stick in the mouth. It is lopsided, like the baby's head is, and the patch of cotton pad that covers the babies open sores make it look like a Father Christmas beard. It could hardly be seen against the redness of Shannon's forehead though, and is only about the size of a ten pence coin.

It is as if it is painted on, in a cartoon style. The nurse discreetly licks her finger and rubs at it, while answering, 'See what? Is she trying to tell you something?' Distraction theft is another habit, and the doctor, on cue, doesn't notice her hand movements. It is a learnt ignorance.

They believe in the power of copying, of aping, and they think that victims will echo them in shock, and strangely, it seems to work, but mostly only on one of themselves.

Eyes glaze, or they are averted from the obvious theft.

Shannon stares, and doesn't signal anything else. The doctor's eyes are bloodshot and he is sweaty. They both smell, and the smell lingers with that of the dead. He is wearing a turban.

She was rubbed, as if she was paper. She is trapped and unable to move away. Her arms and legs do not react to her thoughts and stay limp. She closes her eyes to the two heads that are studying her own decoy one, and feints.

*

Some of the emergency workers are gathering in the hospital cafeteria, for a rest and weak soup, to help their stomachs to stop revolting against the events that they are helping with. The wind is stopping them from moving. It is whisking leafy edges to in to peaks, and squashing them against house walls. The rain is creating waterfalls from drain pipes, and duck ponds from grass. No one is going anywhere.

The doctor and nurse are discussing the baby in an unaccustomed shared tea break. They do not normally socialise, but feel that sitting at a Formica table is appropriate on this occasion. They feel important, and interesting. They have used their mobiles, to take photos while the baby slept. They are printed, and are sitting in a large brown envelope. They have been unable to broadcast or to send any photos with their mobiles though. The phone networks are down. The doctor has looked on the internet for guidance, and found some long words that can be associated with Shannon, that slightly describes her condition; Hemming syndrome, haemifacial microsmia, craniosynotosi. He will drop them into the conversation, and watch the nurse's face for signs of comprehension. There are only a few that remember their in depth training, the rest know it is futile to hope for more than measured medication duties, and forget as soon as the exams are over. The brown envelope lies between them, on the table top. The nurse drinks an American coffee, and the doctor drinks orange juice. He doesn't want to be discovered as a fraud by the nurse, and he watches her carefully. He thinks they make a cinema picture, sitting there with slamming shutters in the background and dampened howls.

The envelope is opened with ceremony and a flourish, in the knowledge they are being watched by the CCTV, and to distract the nurse from himself.

Shannon's head looks three times as large in the photos.

They are genuinely surprised again at the clarity of her birth marks, and notice the shooting star line for the first time. Her whitened mole is to one side. She is white, blue, and red. Her skin is not thick enough to hide the blemishes. She is creepy looking, with one eye smaller than the other, and bald. Also, in this frozen image, she is comically sneering at them, as if she knows they are not as they seem.

The doctors own skin becomes rosy at the thought that she may know about him. He has unwittingly given her the rumour of godliness, of innate knowledge of others, of their thoughts and deeds, before she is a minute old. He is turning a medical complaint in to an epic world wide religion, in, for once, an accidental echo of the past. It is strange, because it is her sneer that has given her this spiritual and holy connection, not her other, more obvious religious looking blemishes.

The nurse is equally, and accidentally, showing signs of a telepathic connection with the baby. Her eyes have been drawn downwards, towards the baby's chest. She is sitting there, eyes blank, staring at the perfectly formed miniature heart that is placed there. The top photo is upside down to her, and the heart looks like an arrow head. A cupid's arrow head, but also, and more importantly, it is aurora. Its earth bound bottom is pointing to the baby's navel.

A stirring of memory makes her think that the baby is a treasure map, but she watched a lot of treasure hunting films while she watched the hospital nurses, so she doesn't know. Her eyes flicker up towards the sleeping ones of the baby. They skim over the moles, and cheeks, idly plotting places and towns. The mini heart mole, the aurora, has a compass hidden in it as a dark cross. The nurse discreetly takes one of the photos from the prints, while she listens to the doctor's diagnostic report of the baby. He is too excited, and his cheeks are rosy as he sweats out medical terms, and she nods blankly at him. She will make her excuses, and will go and have another look at it, the baby. Her phone is itching in her hand. She wants to send the photo to her friends and family. They will have something other than the weather to talk about, later, for a change, when she finishes her shift.

*

Shannon wakes up silently crying. She had heard that tears are taken notice of, and there will be a remedy for her discontent within a few minutes. She will be moved away from her scowling mother, who snarls, sleeps, and snores and be placed in another room. Her mother barks in a spitty impersonation of her ugly child, and tells her so. Her lips are raised in a phlegmy sneer as she throws insults at her. She is dog child, from her ugly dog father. She is a chewed pig head. She is

211

too ugly to be from her womb. She has been swapped already, by the scabby whore nurse.

Her mother is as unpleasant as Shannon's fears were, and just as real. Her eyes are rat like. She wears glasses to make them reflect the light and to hide her appearance. As soon as she had woken up she had picked the glasses out of her bag, and had peered at her. The glasses were shiny reflective mirrors, and there are two babies sneering back at Shannon, as her mother verbally abuses her.

There had been a few moments of shared hatred, and her mother had gone to the corridor, before returning to give her one more look of disgust. 'Lesbian', she had hissed,' you have been inside me already.'

Her mother was doing the opposite of what was expected, because she was not expecting anymore.

Her mother was a fat retard

Then she had slept, and snored.

Her mother had been a shock.

She closes her eyes, and her mind is silent. The snores are loud, and she is small. No one heard her silent protestations, except for the doctor and the nurse, and they had disregarded her. There are people walking past, who have also ignored her. She is unwanted, and uninteresting to the rescuers. They want blood and broken limbs, tragic scenarios and beautiful sad maidens to comfort, she thinks, not a crying baby to listen to. She is unaware that she is not making any noise.

The pregnancy rooms are normally avoided by the volunteers. They are usually cleaner than the other wards, and do not need extra help. The rooms are smiled at, but not entered. The people passing are too laden with germs and disease to go too near the laborious mothers, and their vulnerable babies anyway.

But from her distant cot they seem to be giving hope and taking it away with their casual smiles. Their eyes are wide and glassy with the horror of reality, and they frighten her. They look like manic, unwashed murderers as they block out the light in the gap of the door. They are blood stained with relaxed ignorance, after brushing and kneeling in slightly cleaned floors and are unseeing as they pass by.

Shannon can tell they are Chrystians by their crosses. The crosses are gold and silver, and sit on their chests, hanging off thin, invisible metal chains. She is surprised to see a tiny man on some of the crosses, and in the half light mistakes the figure for a finger. It is a tied together phalange, the top held in place with a twisted, horizontal plaster, with another further down, wrapped around the adjoining knuckle, in a nappy type design.

They rhyme phalange with hang and say the fingers are crossed, with a quick twist of the fingers. They are rhyming slang slags, who hide their crimes with a uniform innocence. If they were good they would have returned her pleading looks instead of staring at her with undisguised, blank disinterest and have jewellery with such blatant symbolism.

The finger on the cross was their Jeasus, smaller than she thought .it would be. It was the size of her own tiny fingers, and she feels an echo of fear as she finds what she thinks is the root of their icon. They are body snatchers and tomb raiders.

They had the first piece of experimental bio engineering –her bleeding finger - as proof of their supremacy in the medical market, displayed as if it was a damaged, mounted, butterfly rescued from a piece of Victoriana. The finger was pinned together in amateur taxidermy as they sold relics of herself to budding students of the grotesque, fresh from a pickling jar. It would have been her

November finger, her ring finger that they had kept, to see whether it bled independently from the body. The blood would have been put in a vial, and herself in a veil, and it would have been electrocuted in Frankenstein impersonation. It was a shrunken Siamese twin that would grow its body, separate from herself, if they excited the blood with electrical waves. They played 'change a letter' with the past, to make them seem more humane to the future. She was in a vial; She was in a veil.

They were still in the corridor, with their finger crosses hung in front of them. Five fingers made a hand, and she saw how they grouped together, bending as one, with the chains invisibly suspending the crosses in the air. All together the crosses made a palmless, disembodied hand, rising out of the ground, as the people tidied the corridor of fallen sheets and tinny trolleys. She expects the name of the dead is engraved on the back of each cross, as a specimen label, or as if it was a make shift grave for the disembodied. If she had a cross it would hang directly in front of her own crossed heart, giving it a distant and mystic twin; it would be thumb, or finger, balanced on the aurora, but never touching it, just like their church building design.

She wonders where she would fit in, in their rituals. Hand on heart, or it is finger on the heart, as if the red mole was pursed lips. It was to say 'I will swear not to say. I cross my heart.' and the finger cross is on the faux heart, to say it for the wearer. The hand on heart is to forbid the unable to, and the finger on there, a hint not to. The mini mouth is gagged already by nature. The hand is a dictatorship for the mute. It has no real power.

It is an ironic statement that puts the hand there or has them clasped together in front of the chest. They are there to catch the words the sacred heart lips would have uttered, and they speak over its silence with prayers. The hands also wait in prayer imitation, to catch the lips taking flight, as if it was a butterfly.

They have layered her up, for their illusions. The finger is laid on its metal insecta skeleton and is nestled against its sacred heart wings. It becomes a two bit flying thing, ready for the convcyer belt to glue it together for flight.

It is not an interpretation anymore, but becomes real to her, as she pieces together words. The church alter lies in the palm of their abstract hand, and her hand body would lie on it. She would be caught in the hand of a glass gloved Neanderthal, which was a King Kong corporation with a feint woman in it's open fist wall, who would squeeze her blood from her. It is there beneath their icon, in the form of a red carpet. The crucifix was exactly what it portrayed, she thought; It was her bony body, displayed for a anatomical lesson, after the life had finally left; her body that showed signs of biped becoming quadpid, or quadpid becoming biped. It was that part of transfiguration that they had studied. The alter is the altered. They would have had dwarfs, giants and hunchbacks on their platform, to cut into. It was forbidden, she thinks, to tell what happened there, in the past and in their church.

She is thinking bloody, as she stares from the gap that the cotton pads have made at the gap the door makes. The Chrystians have passed and have moved silently out of her line of sight. They will go home and pray for the little children, and not be aware of the irony.

They drink the blood of Chryst in their ceremonies, she remembers that she heard, and hid it with poetic languages. Their drinking cup is a womb grail, two handled and crisscrossed with Celtic entrails: A porringer held up, in ceremonial worship of the aurora, ready for the warm, alive blood of the womb, while echoing it.

215

It becomes real to her, as she listens to her surroundings, in her drifty sleep. It is a theatrical autopsy on the alter, as they drain the blood and divide the body to share.

They become the backs of scarabs, in her dreams, with their hands together and right angled arms hiding bumpy chests that are lungs of wings themselves; like lines of insects preying, instead of praying, with their black choir clothes. They are miniscule and chewing on her wrists.

She does not know why they are on their knees but then there are too many reasons all at once, and they make her puke onto her cot sheet. Their prayer pose was the coast of France and Spain. Italy was their legs and feet. England was in front of them, as a person slumbering.

When they are on their knees they are shrunk to a manageable height by being thrown back into childhood. Then they are led backwards in to pre birth compliancy by a pseudo Scandinavian route, which is a mapped penis. Their partners and children were their snowy peaks that drove them backwards into babyhood. The mountains of Norway and Sweden were brides, choir boys and christenings. They imagine they are a land mass, obeying a larger one. Soon they will be France grabbing at the Scandinavian lands when they hold their penises, too scared to urinate in case one of their European relatives suffers because of it. They are being bewitched ready to be switched. On their knees they are the size of children, not able to be found guilty of any crimes. They were Aurora Horis age.

She no longer trusted the Chrystians, as she sweated. She wanted blood tests and x-rays, antibiotics, and fungal cream, not more nightmares. The hospital people had noticed, and had understood, but had walked away. She wasn't normal. Her body had convinced itself of its worldy status, and had grown to fit it. She wanted to

216

know what had happened in their selfish orbit to make her less, or more human, but instead she finds more reasons for distrust.

It is her arm again, that has splayed itself across the cot, ready for needle jabs that grabs at her thoughts. It was true. There were mole marks, as if the needles had been stuck in it already. The star system Orion was there, as was the JC, or St. She hadn't imagined it. She had seen without seeing, and had formed as she was being told of history.

Her mind is trying to explain to her how to move her arm, so that she can raise herself up. Biceps, triceps, and flexors: abductors and flexing. The Sihs oppose the Chrystians, and rise up against them, it says, as she dozes and closes her eyes. It explains with mole definition.

But something is wrong, as she hears the story. It is war or warts that she listens to as she sleeps. They are the groups of people bloodying the streets. They have made religions out of her arm. One reads from the right, the Chrystians do, one reads from the left. They are the Sihs. They have joined the dots together and read the opposite to each other. They hit people like herself over the head with their lack of logic, as they pull and push at the mind. They use the muscles they represent, twisting and pulling themselves to attack. Despite the aggression they outwardly show each other, they are joined together. They are enemies who are friends, to trap the common enemy within the 'v' of their crooked arm, ready to sneak up behind and encircle throats with false accusations. They are twofold and conspiring in their intentions as they oppose as they pull together, to make a people pyramid out of her spotty arm. They will bend it to raise a fist to hit anyone who wants to escape either cult. The humerus bone held high as the violence starts, like they are caveman cartoons. None believers were the enemy.

217

It wasn't beliefs that they were fighting for though. They had no faith, except in money.

She knows it all as she looks for a hero among the chaos.

The religions were a cover for their real interest. They wanted arms. Computer arms; their preoccupation with hers said it all. They had heard a whisper in the air about them, and had clung to her limb, like a leech, in fear of discovery for their plans. They wanted control of central processing units and computer chips. The religions raised money for them and hid their illegal discussions with duplicate meanings and looks. The stained glass windows were still three fingered, but Jaesus was also a symbol of the miracle microchip, that made people as small as a thumb, that gave it voice and communication too. The chip is Jaesus. It is ratio and ruminations as they stared at the statue, as the Sih's stare at the ground and at the yellowed shorthand writing of the long dead secretaries of the wealthy.

The Sihs impersonated the equatorial countries in their prayer, with their head to the floor, and arses raised. They planned to take them all; the Africans and Americans, the Icelanders and Indians, in pyramid accusation. They were looking for pin numbers too, by looking at the space where her dads ankle would be. They were using the tale of the spare rib, to communicate this. They looked in to space, down there, at shin height, faces hidden from cameras, and identity hidden by uniformity, as they planned attack. They had changed the 'rib' to 'pin', and discussed ways and when to procure it, and others.

She knew her dad was there, icon still, long after everyone else had forgotten the oddity of his skin.

Their crouched pose was also China, in an impersonation of a heel. They used their bodies to plan and plot, as they decided to take

Chinese businesses, and IDs, by turning themselves upside down. They would lose their fake tans, by staying on their front, legs and arms tucked in from the suns rays. They will have botox eye lifts, or willingly give themselves conjunctivitis swellings, to have a Chinese look for a while, to fool cameras and customers.

*

The Sihs also talked to the ground because the faux Chrystians talked to the sky. They were claiming to have control of the underground telephone wires already, and the fake Chrystians were claiming to have power over the satellite systems, by looking up. They were planning a take over.

They will invent shares, and companies, in get rich quick schemes where only the investors lose. They will raise and drop hopes and phones with their fairground fist, made of violence and fear. It is an arms war, but only against the public. They are united in their dream of domination and wealth through being a peeping tom.

*

It is a waste of time, Shannon thinks. She should know, she is arm, and hand, listening in on their world with her confused identity.

The military has control of all.

But the criminals think it is all new, as they covet the radio toys. They were plotting, as she stared at her arm, as the wind glassed and sliced bodies, as the roads shut down and the military took over.

They will whisper together, as they are apart. They will sell phones by loyalty and patriotism, and spy on all in the name of safety. Both of the cults belonged to the Horis. They were followers of the aurora palm, spilling blood on its aisle in the claim of worship.

For the fake Chrystians the Jaesus statue is a keen but obvious disguise for their talk. The myth of her marred body is their clothed discussion of stolen computers and thieved pin numbers too. Her

219

bleeding rib, becomes pin, as they elongate and shorten letters. The word 'number' is made up from a slight stare under the rib, or the colour of the statue. It is umber. Under rib or umber nib, it still means number pin or pin number. Jeasus is a mobile phone, and sins become sims. He is a three inch screen, as they stare at the floor, then exchange numbers by leaving looks in the corners of each others eyes.

*

The Sihs are also claiming to be all of her arm, with their name. It swallows up the JC, backwards, and hints in ugly intent. They will control the Chrystians by their name. They have the power of words to dominate and extract fear. They want the B trail; the line 13 and its towns, its countries. They want it all. They want the sky, and the earth, and everything in between. They want the web spaces, and Google. They want Ebay and bank logins, as they hack through bodies and computer programmes. They have gone mad in greed. They are attacking, as the weather strikes, as the lightening knocks and locks the same systems they are struggling to gain control of.

*

Everyone used her dad's skin for code, because they had been told to. The television had told them to do it, in subtle manipulation of the eyes. The army was a pimp, for her father's and hers private timings and pain. They wanted to know what the criminal planned, and had given them all the same cryptic alphabet to use, so they would know what they were witnessing.

Her dad was father to the stigmata, in a way, or kin to it in skin and bio chemical chain reaction. It was a cycle of genetic, and code inheritance that was being displayed. The army used the stigmata, then they used her father, then they used the stigmata again. It was twofold in its purpose; they could watch the open, unintentional confession of the enemy, and could analyse any further developments of what they called' intelligent' skin, as they displayed the stories on the television. The stories were localised, they were international. The army watches and tells everyone so, by calling the tiny cpu's 'Arms'. They were honest, they implied, watching the dishonest.

The dishonest will discover a new code, once they have been caught, and the new code will be the latest development of the skin, or the oldest. The army will tell them what code to use, so they can catch them again.

.*

She is soothsayer, and a late prophet to tell the world of Sih intentions, just as her father was too late in his warnings to the world. She had to tell him before they got him too. His cheap, expensive phone was GPS ed. It had belonged to his double, who they had already murdered. They had slipped it out of a cold hand into a warm one, ready to blame him for the theft of it, and the life they took, should they be caught. They did not know why he was different from others, but it would not matter if his wife was willing to lie. She would be.

She knew it as she lay there, helpless.

The Sihs and Chrystians, that were Horis, were joined in blood. They were brothers and sisters, cousins and kin, disguising their relationships with differing skin tones. They were blonde, red headed, brunette, brown and black. They will betray each other for fun, for drama, and for money. Blood is less noticeable on darker skin, and the more tanned ones are the ones that have been persuaded to kill, in the darkness.

They had taken the television, and the newspapers. They had stolen them with the riots and the hurricanes, with anonymous names and faces, in a timed attack. The Horis had taken control by stealing laptops and passwords, phones and pin numbers. They had swept the wealthy from the land with fake email invites from addresses that were familiar and trusted. They had tempted in the rich with past videos of family or friends on hacked intercoms. They had bugged and burgled the influential while the storms had raged, and while the electricity had been cut off. It had happened all over the world.

They had taken everyone, from top to bottom. They had stabbed kin and lovers to get there, as they believed their own publicity and had started a war with themselves.

*

And the military had been waiting for them. It is total shut down and freeze frame. Caught and clouted. Over, and over again. The television and newspaper are frozen eternity and never evolving, because of the Horis, the military say, as they confiscate estates and dismantle gangs. They had let them kill and had reaped the awards.

It happened the night before she was born.

*

But it hadn't just been the Horis. She knew.

The military had nearly realised too late what the intentions of their own programmers had been. The programmers were the ones that controlled the media with an intellectual hand, and kept the masses in control. They were the testers of bias and brain washing; to stop either happening. Something had gone wrong.

They had, they said, re taught the Horis. Assimilate to alienate, as asked to do. They had used the corners and spaces of the TV screen to re-teach the cults, using their own love of silence, and secrecy, corners, angles and pyramids. They had manipulated film, so characters looked their message out.

222

But it was worse, and it was happening as she listened, as the final shut down for every media is locked into place; as the satellites are isolated, and frozen into orbit; as important phone lines are cut off from every computer operated machine.

The programmers had decieved. They had used the corncrs and spaces of the TV screen to program androids and computers in a distant manipulation.

The army had been looking in the wrong place when they had looked for robot activity. The programmers had used a binary code, in a slow but steady message, in the same looks that had been targeted to the Horis. It was a one, two look, like the code that sent the person back to the womb they grew in, to be re taught, that turned the switches of the CPUs off and on.

The Horis had been a cover; a threat that had been exaggerated, for their own subversive actions, but had grown again, in accidental or purposeful recruitment.

The programmers will be millionaires, and all powerful, as the androids slip into place, as the computers play back instructions at unbelievable speeds, and relate instructions. They had used the satellites to reflect images into the clouds, with the same veiled visual commands, for the machines that were solar powered controlled. They had claimed it had been a natural phenomenon, in response to radio active air and beamed movies, when asked by the slightly environmentally concerned.

It was lucky that media is not weaponry, as everyone would have been dead, just before she had been born.

The army had caught the robot activity on searching computers, after looking at the directions the Horis had been given. They had fed the TV through code-breaking software, and had watched with alarm as their own computers had started to react.

They didn't have any codes to stop them. The androids were invisible to searching radar, in the jumble of machines that kept the world going.

If the military turned the internet and wifi communication off to find them, they wouldn't be able to find them. The world would also stop, and their own computer emergency systems would fail. The safest and only way to proceed was to repeat the same programmes, the same newspapers, and the same radio, to take the human-looking machines back to the beginning, of the loop of commands that were being obeyed.

It is a flurried blur of activity as army scientists play with the heated keyboards, and realisation dawns on why the media machine had been stopped in the first place.

*

It is the doctor and nurse that wake Shannon up again. They are thumbing their mobiles still, like they are mechanical and on a loop. The little boxes flash; as if they are two of the three kings of the nativity scene, come to visit her, bearing gifts. It is him, in a centuries old turban that gives the impression of antiquity. He is carrying a box of Myrror, which is his flashing mobile. He will be sending her image across the world using satellites that bear the same name too, to his homeland in Asia, The nurse is carrying gold, because that is the colour of her hair, and the colour of the light that blinds Shannon's eyes as the flash operates.

Shannon is the other box of treasure. She is frankincense, which is the essence of Frankenstein. She is the king that carries herself, and the only one that wears a crown.

224

The nativity stars, all in the same room, for the pleasure of the CCTV cameras. They are stood to one side of the cot, and her mother is on the other. She has stopped snoring, and is echoing silence instead.

Shannon is carrying her holy parents within her. Her father is a carpenter wasp, and her mother is her Verge. Her audience of animals are herself; she has the features of them all, with her dog ears, while she lies in her manger.

*

'I want paying for that.' Her mother, who has been watching them from her bed, has interrupted the amateur photographers with the sleazy demand. The hospital blanket is wrapped around her; it is a crowd scene dress from the same nativity play. She is like a plastic figural from a Christmas set, fallen over.

'Why are you taking photos of it for anyway? It aint ugly enough for the papers.'

They are red and silent, as they stare at her mother. They know she does not know. The asian doctors eyes flicker towards the nurse, who responds to her mothers question with a practised even tone.

'They are for hospital records. She has a slightly larger skull on one side. It has to be documented. I am afraid we can not pay you for any photographs we take. They will not be publicised.' The nurse pauses for a second or two, before lowering her voice. 'The baby may not last the night. We are praying for her.'

Shannon is stunned back to sleep. She has feinted, and will leave a faint outline when she has died. She may not last for another few hours. She has no oxygen mask to help her, or doctors standing by to resuscitate her. She will be dead and gone, put in to a clear plastic sack and carried with over-large tweezers. She will be slipped under the sheets of the dead in the corridor, and put into an emergency mass grave.

She wants to live.
Her feet move in a kicking motion, unseen, and arms flail.

*

The nurse has decided the future for the ugly child. The baby will not be missed by the mother, so she will be taken in by her family. Shannon will make them money, and give them amusement, instead of giving that hag either.

There is a festival for the aurora on its *M.* day, November 14th, which is a few months away. It is a lazy day, to match the bleed. Everyone is woman for a while before and afterwards. It used to be months, and still is for some, but mostly now it is a long weekend, of three days. Twenty four hours either side of the *M.* day. Six sets of twelve hours, altogether, for six years of menstruation. And on the count of seven, she, who is both sexes, made heaven, and the steps to it.

Seven Horis years was eighty four years of age. That is if they are gods and goddesses. Mere mortals like her were one side of the event, and lasted half way through the actual day. She would be three years old, thirty six. The male was the other side, metaphorically speaking, and would last the same. They met in the middle, to make the aurora. Together they were twelve. 3+3+6+6 = 12.

The baby might take her place, if they chose it, rather than her, and she would be moved up in the ladder of success. She would become closer to goddess status.

*

She has forgotten the doctor standing next to her. The words had slipped out unintentionally, without forethought or planning. It was the shock of being caught, and the mood of disasters and drama that had made the words form. She was taking an opportunist chance. The baby was tiny, any how, and may die.

226

The doctor has laid a dramatic hand on the shoulder of the nurse. It is comforting rather than insulting. If he wanted to insult her, he would have laid a hand on her elbow, to say that was where her hand should have been. It was gesture to turn the elbow to a paw, and was accompanied by a pitiful look. Poor you: paw you. Some, those that called themselves beetles and ants, gently touch the shoulder, to get attention. They called women maggots and mother. The turban was the fake worshipper's maggot vagina. They used it for propaganda war against their doubles.

This is the touch he has used, as if she was maggot mother, who possessed no arms, and him the sympathetic new born, stuck, as Shannon thought she would be, between the legs. He was acting at being the innocent full grow son, wanting to be in his mother again, and claiming he never really left. He was attached still, by his shaved vagina hat. He is a son possessed by dark thoughts, and jealousy of her partner, with planned and fake immaturity.

The gesture is another television direction, which is planned to reveal feelings and thoughts of the person who will fit himself into the action. It is betrayal of the father, who feeds him, that the army want summed up and said in a charade. It means a threatening gesture towards themselves, because they are the ones that feed him; he wants to put his hand over the soldiers' mouth too. The soldiers' mouth is shown as the heart, that sits on Shannon's shoulder, in another televised fable, and he wants to shut it up.

It is a gesture of complicity that the fake doctor has offered. He will take the child to the squat he shares, and see whether there is anyone who will want the corpse, should she die, for study. It is an unusual skin complaint. He may be able to sell it for more then he hoped, with the photos to accompany it, if she is to die anyway. He thinks the nurse knows more than him.

Their morals have all spilt out, after her mother revealed hers. The nurse has conceded that she is a liar, and thinks the doctor has agreed to lie with her, using swift lizard type looks. There is a slight sense of relief in the air, now they think they are among friends. It can't be seen in their words or gestures, but can be felt.

Her mother has already regretted the words that she has uttered that might make her lose her other children, to the social workers, but, for no reason at all, knows that it won't go any further. It is the life and death situation of the atmosphere outside that has made her rash. The thin veneer that keeps her on the side of civilisation is being stripped away, and she gets ready for niceties that hold it together to disappear. She has watched the nurses and doctors change over the years, and know they are the same as she is. She thinks she is less of a criminal, more humane than they are though. She didn't take the 'acting' jobs that they did. She would never pick up her knife, and pretend it was a scalpel. She wouldn't steal scenes from an afternoon TV programme, which starred fictitious characters and ink blood, to act out in the watched white corridors of the hospital. She would not stalk, not like they did anyhow, and try to nurse people like herself to health, without knowing even the basics. They were insane for money, while she was just clever. She earnt more from her children in a week than they earnt in a month.

But, she had reasoned with herself, if they could get away with doing nothing for money, then one of her children could too.

She took a photo of the nurse, as the doctor and nurse turned their attention to the baby. She would see if one of hers would match her. It didn't matter about the toilet fish, which was going to be flushed anyway. She would be able to get two hundred pound funeral expenses and still have the birth certificate.

*

228

While Shannon is unconscious, she is moved. The cot has wheels, and she is pushed, like the dead people and her mother, through the morgue corridors.

They will place her in a separate room, on the pretext of imminent death, and she will think it is true. She believes nurses; they are good people, who help the ill. She will stop breathing if she has enough faith in the nurse's words. Her breathes will become shorter. She will divide each one by ten, to make it smaller with each inhale, and exhale, until it disappears, along with herself. She is Pavlov's dog again, shrunk to the size of a pole cat, and then to a size of a Cheshire cat, before finally resting as a simile and a lab rat, taking a last and first sniff at washed clothes.

They had lost though, her mothers friends had, and she was glad. They will arrest her mother, when they get the time, or sterilise her with the acid from her own spiteful words, and Shannon won't care because she has already lived.

.